Daughter of Sarpedon

An Anthology Edited by Heather and
S.D. Vassallo

Daughter of Sarpedon

Dedicated to the unjustly treated who survived to tell their own stories (and those who didn't who we will never forget).

Content warnings are provided at the end of this book.

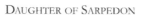

Contents

A Toast. © 2022 Elizabeth Leggett. All rights reserved.

Foreword

In 1997, I read an article by Dr. Ann Scales titled *Disappearing Medusa: The Fate of Feminist Legal Theory?** In this article are two lines that I have kept on a notecard ever since:

"In short, Medusa is the unvarnished, undomesticated-and incomplete-counternarrative to patriarchy. Medusa represents the possibility of a transformatively different consciousness."

To say these particular lines had a significant impact on me at the time, would be an unbelievable understatement. All these years later, they still do.

Heather Vassallo
September 2022

*Scales, Ann. "Disappearing Medusa: The Fate of Feminist Legal Theory?" *Harvard Women's Law Journal,* vol. 20, 1997, pp. 34–45.

Introduction

by Tracey Fahey

You only have to look at the Medusa straight on to see her. And she's not deadly. She's beautiful and she's laughing. (Cixous, (1976) The Laugh Of The Medusa, p885)

In, *Daughter of Sarpedon*, Brigid's Gate, with their staunch history of revoicing mythological characters, collate a range of responses to Medusa. They do this through the medium of forty-eight collected short stories, poetry and drabbles that, in their different ways, try to articulate the multiple meanings of Medusa's complex character. In Alyson Faye's 'Circus of Shadows,' the ringleader Bascalus' asks us 'Myth or Monster? Goddess or Gorgon?' And well he might.

Medusa is many things; she is manipulated, she is deadly, but also, as Cixous points out, 'she's beautiful and she's laughing.'

Myths return to contemporary culture for a reason; to address modern problematics using the old language. Medusa looms above us, snake-tentacled, a disruptor of our ideas about human relationships, betrayal and revenge. Her story is a difficult one; she moves through it from Gorgon, a protector, to subject of patriarchal abuse, to object of fear, to murder victim. Medusa, herself a hybrid, is a liminal being, suspended between fear and desire, good and evil, monster and human. In putting this anthology together, Heather and S.D. Vassallo have ably curated a wide range of re-imaginings that capture the many nuances of this wounded but powerful woman, this survivor, this storyteller.

Medusa is many things. For millennia, she has been a muse. We can trace her evolution in writing, through the work of Homer, Ovid and Hesiod. She is also an intensely visual concept. In 2018, an exhibition opened in the Metropolitan Museum of

Art, Manhattan, Dangerous Beauty: Medusa in Classical Art. From ancient Greek culture she is first represented by the terracotta figure of a tusked and bearded monster dating from 570BC, one of the last icons of her a symbol of luxury, the Versace label. As we move from the Archaic to the Classical and Hellenistic periods and towards the present day, a shift occurs, from monstrosity to humanity, echoing Medusa's mortal origins, moving towards the beautiful snake-tentacled icon we recognise today. Of all the representations, perhaps the most haunting are Caravaggio's iconic versions of Medusa (the first in 1596 and the second in 1597). Remember that Sigmund Freud in his Das Medusenhaupt (Medusa's Head) of 1940 saw the act of decapitation as akin to the act of castration, where the fear apparent in the Gorgoneion (the Gorgon head) is linked to the sight of something. In these images the Medusa is presented as self-portrait; her startled face becomes a mirror in which the ghost of the artist's own traumatic life is glimpsed. Here Caravaggio recognise the Medusa in himself; victim, monster, and yet with the agency of self-representation.

In *Daughter of Sarpedon*, forty-eight writers explore what Medusa has meant and continues to mean in contemporary culture. Medusa is many things. And some of these make difficult reading. In the original myth, she is a mortal woman with two immortal sisters, born of sea-creatures Phorcys and Ceto; together they are the Gorgons. But according to Roman poet Ovid (Metamorphoses 4.794–803), she becomes a hand-maiden to Athena (later Minerva) and is assaulted by Nepture, the Roman version of Poseidon. This status of innocent victim is one way to reimagine Medusa; in the poem 'Such Secrets, These Stones' by Stephanie Wytovich she writes movingly of Medusa's plight: 'Your eyes an hourglass of erased/ Legacies, the laughter of swordfish/ An open wound screaming/Between my legs.' Christina Bagni's protagonist in 'The Snakes We Feed,' a moving, visceral narrative of abuse, pain, denial and confusion, hides a snake under her hat and a darker secret in her heart. 'I could feel the ends of its muscles moving in me, like a fetus, like a parasite, like a tumour with tentacles.' But there is also anger here—in the beautiful story, 'Snakes and Stones', Claire McNerney is forthright in her exhortation to Medusa to invert the narrative of victimization: "'Yes, I am hideous. Yes, I am unlovable. Yes, I brought this upon myself." As if it was her fault her uncle took her to the temple that day and let the gods open her up and leave her hollow.' The fierceness of this narrative reminds us that today the Medusa tattoo has become a symbol of power for victims of sexual assault; by assimilating the identity of Medusa, they rewrite the history of victim-shaming.

Medusa is many things. She is also a survivor. There is a clarity to her vision. As Athena says in Laura Kaschak's 'Shedding Skin'—"'Ah, but haven't you learned yet? The woman is always blamed for the man's crimes against her." In 'Medi's Dance,' Medusa blends effortlessly into New York life—'She had made it this far because she was strong, smart and resilient. She was a survivor.' And, as a survivor, she is also poised for revenge.

In the Prelude to this collection, 'An Ode to the Stone-Cold Gaze,' Eva Papasoulioti writes: 'Sometimes poems are like snakes; they slither and hiss in your head until they offer to bite you. Revenge blooms in ripples. Our snakes sing songs to the ocean.' A fitting note to strike, for later, in 'The Ayes Have It' by Gordon Linzner, Margaret Duchet haunts the Victorian court of the Old Bailey, meting out justice to men who harm women. In 'Set in Stone,' Owl Goingback reimagines Medusa on a virtual app, revealing herself to predatory men in an act of revenge. 'You beg to see all of me/And I let the shadows fall away.' However, interestingly, in Sam Muller's 'She Who Roams Far,' Medusa's sister Euryale recognises the freedom that eschewing revenge can bring. 'Hate and fear create and sustain belief. You can't hate what you don't believe in; you can't fear what you don't believe in.' Sometimes, the ultimate act of revenge is to speak the truth, to inscribe a female testimony. As Cixous puts it: 'A feminine text cannot fail to be more than subversive. It is volcanic; as it is written it brings about an upheaval of the old property crust, carrier of masculine investments; there's no other way. There's no room for her if she's not a he.' (p.888)

In *Daughter of Sarpedon*, the image of Medusa also functions to critically examine the idea of the hero-narrative espoused by writers from Homer to Joseph Campbell. Thomas Joyce's 'No

God's Country, No Man's Land,' offers us a Western-inspired tale of justice that questions the concept of hero, while Die Booth's trans protagonist, Melissa in 'Leaving Athens Street,' resolutely expels her unpleasant landlord Percy: "'You're not the hero anymore." Melissa says, as the three of them back him out of the door. "Things are changing, and this is only the beginning.'"

In questioning this hero-narrative, the writers of this anthology also explore the meaning of true monstrosity. As Elizabeth Detzler puts it in 'Gorgon's Gaze,'—'She may look like a monster, but she knew only true monsters ever saw a gorgon's gaze.' Meanwhile, Marshall J. Moore, in 'First,' offers Medusa's weary narration as a harassed woman: 'The man following me home is not the first to do so, not even close…There is no difference between he and I, save one. I did not choose to be who I am.' In 'Don't Tell Me to Smile,' Kristin Cleaveland engages a clever use of a pandemic backdrop as metaphor for the masks we need, as a man in a pharmacy insolently asks Medusa: 'Why don't you take that thing off? Stop living in fear?' But he is the real threat, the real monster, which she deals with. Efficiently.

For Medusa's narrative is not a simple one of victim. She also has agency. Even when she doesn't speak, as in SJ Townend's short but powerful 'Ghosted,' her silence provokes Poseidon to blind himself with the aid of Lamia to win her heart. Her sole response? 'Medsss@Poseidon: YOU ARE BLOCKED FROM FOLLOWING '@MEDSSS'.' But her agency does not just extend to herself, she is a protector.

Let's contemplate the Gorgoneion again, that icon of Medusa's decapitated head. This image has functioned throughout history as an apotropaic amulet, protective, akin to the symbol of the Evil Eye. In these stories, Medusa's desire to save shines bright. Catherine McCarthy's hero, Dussy, for example, rescues snakes in 'Sanctuary': 'The viper coils, then rests its head against her thumb pad. "Poor baby," she says. "Let's get you fixed, hey?" The vertical slits of its pupils are milky; its tail misshapen and bloody.' But for the most part, in this anthology, there attention here is focused on protecting women.

There are no recorded accounts of Medusa turning women to stone; and in this range of stories and poems, she is transmuted into an active protector of women. The mermaid-figureheads in 'Jellyfish' by Avra Margariti are unharmed by Medusa: 'They swim around her, a seafoam-skinned/Shoal immune to her potent power.' In Laura Kaschak's narrative of 'Shedding Skin' the image of the fractured rock she focuses on during her assault becomes intertwined with her new powers as petrifying monster. 'Each one I add makes the world a safer place for women. Each stone I create fills a little more of the fracture within me. I will not be the one to crumble.'

For women, she represents safety, but also love, as in 'The Coming of Perseid' by April Yates. In this short piece, Medusa reaches out to the woman come to slay her: 'That must be why they have sent this girl in her ill-fitting armour. Who drops her sword, shivering and moaning, when I caress her. Yes, I turn men into stone, but it seems I turn women into water.'

Even when Medusa displays a seeming monstrosity towards women, she has a deeper motive as in the shocking 'Gods and Other Monsters.' Rachel Dempsey's tale tells of a woman whose boyfriend attempts to assault a girl, who then turns her knife on the victim: 'The blade, so light in my hand, slid through her skin as smoothly as a snake through water.' Crucially, she means her victim no harm, which is fully recognised in the narrative: 'That girl. She came to visit me. Face all sewn up with shiny pink scars like a hideous doll. It must have hurt to smile, but how her skin stretched, how her teeth flashed, when she saw me behind the glass.' Medusa still wants to protect.

In Renée Meloche's dark and imaginative 'Monstrous Birth' she writes:

'I took the name Medusa, so the world would know me for what I had become. The guardian—protector of these cliffs, these dark woods. This world that relegates its monsters to the dark corners. The ruler of my will, my desire, my fate. The sinuous, twining quality of my nature apparent for all to see—from she to slithering they.'

In this story the power of Medusa blazes, they own their own craving, though Poseidon warns 'Desire is a monstrous thing.' They are even compassionate towards those who come to vanquish them: 'From salt and air and water, I remade men into stone; heroes preserved at the height of their glory, forever.' They even take agency in death.

'See Medusa lunge forward, their scaled coils taut with muscle seething, then surging and snapping. They snatch the hero's sword, holding it aloft. "My goddess Athena, I dedicate this birth to you! Let the world behold my children in their monstrous forms, my will and my desire entwined with the gods'. Let them reshape the world, so that the stories of gods and monsters—our stories—may never be forgotten."'

Let us pause there. As we keep repeating (and it bears repeating) Medusa is many things. For Hélène Cixous in The Laugh Of The Medusa, she became a metaphor for the imperative of women to write and tell their stories: 'Woman must put herself into the text—as into the world and into history—by her own movement.' (1976, p.875) While Lyndsey Croal rightly recognises the historic desire for male narratives in her 'A Heart Turned to Stone'—'No one wants to hear that story. They only want the other, of the man that long ago broke her, and turned her heart to stone'—this anthology excels in contemplating the weight of story and the importance of revoicing female narratives.

In 'The Original Nasty Woman,' Theresa Derwin's Medusa rescues a girl from unwanted male attention in a cinema during Clash of the Titans: '"It is okay," I tell her. "History is told by the victors. And of course, they do not call it his-story for nothing."' This tension between his-story and her-story is maintained in 'Stone Against the Sea' by Elyse Russell where Medusa speaks:

"For years, I have listened. Muffled, through the sides of this box, I've heard the voices of generations of mortals. I've been placed on mantles for decoration; I've been stored in warehouses and attics. And I've heard them tell my story to their children on more than one occasion. But they've always gotten it wrong…"

Similarly, in 'A Bedtime Story' Deborah Markus's Medusa says scornfully to a man with his eyes shut in fear of her: 'You'd rather believe some stranger's tale than take my word about my own life? Typical. Men write stories. Women have to live them. And when the lives don't match the stories, we're the ones who must be doing it wrong.' But in this story, in this anthology, Medusa rights this wrong, she reclaims her narrative and her autonomy. As

Cixous puts it: 'By writing her self, woman will return to the body which has been more than confiscated from her, which has been turned into the uncanny stranger on display.' (p880)

Medusa is many things. Even in the seemingly-unconnected lagniappe, 'The Octavia' by Agatha Andrews, where the figurehead soul of the ship haunts the former captain ('the only ghost he couldn't outrun'), as her wooden self rises, plaything turned to nemesis, we see in her the ghost of Medusa, taken by sea-god Poisedon. And of course, it's also a delicate reminder that of the female sea-creatures already drifting to the surface of the forthcoming Brigid Gate anthology, *Dangerous Waters: Deadly Women of the Sea.*

For now, let us take our leave of the Medusa; victim, creature of power and agency, monster, protector, narrator, in the sure and certain knowledge that she has been fully, thoughtfully and lovingly reimagined here by these stories, poems and drabbles. And as you shut the book, listen for the faint, plaintive echo of siren song, a promise of the future as Brigid's Gate continue their mission to revisit classical mythologies, and in doing so, to celebrate and re-position the unvoiced and the marginalised.

Snake Charmer. © 2022 Winter Ross. All rights reserved.

Prelude

An Ode to the Stone Cold Gaze

by Eva Papasoulioti

They say gods aren't good with words; they aren't good with people either. We're Medusa, mother of monsters, murderer of men, miswritten mortal.

Innocence is a word as heavy as the sea is deep and rocks unbendable. Drop a stone in the water—no human is untethered from divine spit.

Sometimes poems are like snakes; they slither and hiss in your head until they offer to bite you. Revenge blooms in ripples. Our snakes sing songs to the ocean.

Men become rocks in the still of an eye. Eternal gift from a goddess. From woman to woman, weapon against powerlessness. Our voice is wind. Our choice breaking bone.

We kiss earth in cold blood of insolent lips. You make lovers, you make enemies. Gods made us word for word, an astronomical order behind heroes and verses.

We're Medusa. Monster from mortal—to be murdered by man attached to the gods' strings. So go ahead, man, tell us, will you make a poem out of us?

BOOK I

Shedding Skin

by Laura G. Kaschak

I never knew being a monster could feel so good. I suffered their piercing stares my entire life. Now they will be the ones to suffer if they dare look my way. I feel safe for the first time. I enjoy a quiet peace that only comes from solitude and the knowledge that no one can ever violate my sanctuary. Once again, I silently thank the goddess Athena for giving me this gift.

Everyone thinks they know about it, but they don't grasp its true nature. She turned me into the most feared, hideous creature in all of Greece. Men tremble at the thought of facing the infamous Medusa.

Where I once had silken flesh that all men longed to touch, I am now covered in rough scales that surge with venom. People don't grasp how this transformation could feel like anything but a curse, and that is how she and I planned it to appear. They might see the truth if they had been there that notorious day. If they could know what beauty brought me, they might understand how I could now revel in this gruesome form.

I've never known what it's like to walk through the world unnoticed. No one should be forced to grow up too fast just to withstand the expectations of strangers as I had to. The innocence of childhood that most others are allowed to enjoy was stripped for me because of something I had no control over.

When I was still young enough to be seen as cute, it was possible to think of the smiles from strangers as kindness. But as my womanly shape began to form, I noticed a change in those smiles. The men began to let their looks linger a bit longer. Their eyes seemed to take in more of me, making me feel exposed no matter how many layers I wore. They would still give me a smile but now hiding within it was something dark and secretiv something I couldn't understand at such a young age. You'd think my tender age would protect me. It should have repelled the men but instead it seemed to encourage them.

The women's smiles changed, too. No longer did they tilt their heads towards me with a wide toothy grin and kind eyes. Now the smiles were quick and thin lipped. Their chins nudged upwards and their eyes squinted just a bit. It was obvious they disapproved of something but I didn't know what that could be.

Eventually, a terrible incident in the market showed me exactly what was in those disapproving looks. A seller called me over with a kind smile. I had no reason to be suspicious and I didn't want to be rude. I went right over to him. He offered me a free peach as we laughed and chatted. I was lost in the cheerful conversation and didn't notice his wife approaching. I also did not see the handful of dirt the woman carried until it was thrown directly into my face. I was so stunned and confused, it took me a moment to realize the woman had called me a vile, degrading name before roughly yanking her husband away.

I was left standing alone, all eyes turned my way yet again. Heat filled my face as I fought back tears. Continuing my shopping was unimaginable. I hurried away from their stares as fast as I could.

Before I could make it home, the humiliation washed over me in a tidal wave that knocked me to my knees.

I found myself at the base of a tree, sobbing as if I could wash away the shame with tears. It was at this moment that the goddess Athena first introduced herself to me. It's not every day that a goddess appears to a mortal. The sight of her interrupted my lament.

"Jealousy will bring the worst out of people every time," Athena said with a kind voice. "Even the gods are too often possessed by it."

I stared dumbly for a moment before registering her words. Blinking away tears, I told her, "I didn't do anything wrong. If she believes her husband would have inappropriate intentions towards every girl he speaks to, he should be the one she throws dirt at. He is the one deserving of her wrath."

Athena cast her head downward and slowly shook it back and forth. "Ah, but haven't you learned yet? The woman is always blamed for the man's crimes against her."

This simple truth was no real surprise. Life experiences had proven this to me over and over again. Yet hearing it said so plainly stunned me for a moment. And though I knew it to be a fact, I could not fathom the reason for this inequality. I thought a goddess might be able to give me new insight and so I asked her, "Why do you think it's this way?"

With a sly smirk and an arch of an eyebrow Athena replied, "Because men are the weaker sex of course. How can we expect them to have self-control or principles when they are so feeble minded and weak willed? Of course, the burden falls to the women. So much more is expected of us because we are capable of so much more."

That sarcastic tone was all it took to win my heart. We burst into laughter at the same time. Soon, the muscles in my cheeks and stomach ached from the hilarity.

A special bond was formed between goddess and mortal in that one conversation. It became a regular part of the week to meet at that tree for private discussions.

Athena is the goddess of war and wisdom. She has always been known as the most levelheaded of all the gods and goddesses. Vanity and jealousy are silly ideas to her and she refuses to waste time with them.

As the virgin goddess, she had taken a vow of chastity. I was not seen by her as competition the way other women or even goddesses would view me. Athena was also no stranger to the injustices women endure and so we would often commiserate about surviving in a patriarchal world.

It seemed our spot together at the tree was the one place, above or below, where we could both feel truly free of society's expectations or judgments.

Athena was the only one who understood my frustrations and the reasons I turned down every vain, loathsome suitor. She came to me one day with a solution.

"Be my priestess," Athena said.

I had not expected such a suggestion and was a little confused at first how that would solve my problems.

"As a virgin goddess, I must be served by a priestess who has also taken a vow of chastity. Once you take your vows, no man may touch you. All these ridiculous suitors will be forced to give up the chase. The women will no longer see you as competition. In serving me, the burdens of your physical form will be lifted."

I could see no flaw in her logic. Picturing a life in quiet prayer and conversation with Athena filled me with a sense of relief I'd never experienced. I eagerly made a vow to serve in Athena's temple as a virgin priestess.

The days slipped by effortlessly as I settled into the tranquility of life as a priestess. People treated me with a new respect. My duties were simple. I oversaw sacred ceremonies and led the daily rituals of worship. But most of my time was spent caring for the statue of Athena, polishing marble, cleaning the temple, and making sure our supply of offerings stayed full. I could have spent the rest of my life in that temple, losing myself in the mundane.

I'm sure many people would see it as a boring existence; people don't know boredom is a luxury. Exciting lives are full of painful surprises. Given a choice, I'd choose boredom over drama.

But that choice was stolen from me by a god named Poseidon.

Everyone knew about Poseidon. His hot temper and violent nature provided many entertaining stories. I never had reason to believe I would meet him. Little did I know, stories of my beauty and vow of chastity had made their way as far as the heavens. This made me an irresistible prize to someone like Poseidon. His arrogance and unchecked desires drove him to Athena's temple in search of me. And it was in the stillness of that temple that he did find me. I was humming quietly to myself as I tidied the altar from the day's rituals. If I had known it would be the last time I would serve as priestess, I would have savored those moments more. The quiet was shattered by the sound of Poseidon saying my name. My entire world was shattered by him moments later.

I won't describe what he did to me. Too many women already know the details. There is enough of that kind of suffering in the world. I refuse to add more, even with words.

It's strange where your thoughts go during something like that. My body was trapped and powerless so I guess my mind was tasked with shielding any other part of me. I turned my head away and noticed a small crack in the base of a pillar near me.

I focused on that fracture until it was all I could see. I would need to tend to it as soon as possible. You can't ignore that kind of damage even if no one else sees it. It weakens the marrow and threatens to crumble everything if left uncared for.

I clung to the sight of it as he prepared to leave. I wanted to hide inside the darkness of that wounded stone but was instead left vulnerable on the temple floor, stripped bare of more than my clothing. I laid on the cold, hard marble for what could have been minutes, hours, or days. I hadn't come back to myself yet. I didn't really want to. Coming back to my body would mean thinking about what had happened and all that it meant. So, I kept staring at that crack in the pillar, willing it to open wide and swallow me whole.

A sudden gasp reached my ears through the fog. I looked up to see Athena. Suddenly my senses came rushing back and I discovered I was crying.

Knowing she saw me in that state filled me with unbearable shame. She must have seen me as a torn and broken porcelain doll tossed to the floor like forgotten trash.

That is how I saw myself.

She rushed to my side and I could see in her eyes all the urgent questions she wanted answers to. Always the wise goddess, she knew not to press me just then.

Without another word, she gently covered my exposed, raw flesh with the discarded shreds of my clothing. Her strong hands carefully helped me to sit up and she began tending to my wounds. I could feel the love in her touch but I knew even then that there would forever be wounds deep inside that she could never heal for me. My body was soon clean of the blood and dirt from the temple floor but I couldn't really feel clean. I'd never feel clean again. Poseidon's forceful touch would not be so easily washed away.

We sat together in the stillness. I have never been so grateful for anything like I am for those quiet moments Athena let me have. Finally, I tried to find my voice. My throat burned and the muscles clenched tight as I searched for the words that could convey what I had just experienced. I only managed to whisper one word. It came out so quietly, I was sure she didn't hear it.

"Poseidon …"

I felt every muscle in her go rigid and knew immediately that she did hear me. I didn't need to say anything else for her to understand the entire story. Her teeth clenched and body began to tremble. Soon, even the walls of the temple were rumbling with her outrage.

"He did this to my friend, my priestess, in my own temple." She spoke in a deceptively calm tone that displayed more rage than any scream could have done.

After so many years in each other's confidence, I knew exactly what she was thinking about doing. I could not permit it to happen.

"You can't go after him for this. It would mean war among the gods."

"War is what I do best," she growled.

I pleaded with her. "You know that all the gods and goddesses would be against you. Not one will agree a mortal woman is worth

24

your attack on Poseidon. They would make sure all of Athens suffers for your insolence. If that happens in my name, I'd never be able to live with the guilt. Please, don't put that on me. You are the goddess of war and yes, war is what you do best. But you are also the goddess of wisdom. You must see there is no wisdom in open rebellion that's doomed to fail."

It would have been understandable for her to carry on in a rage. Instead, she seemed to swallow her pride and anger. Her head bowed down in quiet agreement. I had never seen my friend's shoulders slumped in defeat before. I don't think she knew what to do or how to help at that moment.

So, she did the only thing she could. She held my hand and listened. She listened as I released all the thoughts that were poisoning me.

"What can become of me now? Where can I go? I have been defiled. I can no longer serve as your priestess. No man would have me as his wife after this. Even the women will be merciless. They will insist I brought this on myself. I will carry the shame that belongs to that loathsome libertine, Poseidon. He will not face the slightest retribution or even embarrassment over his actions."

Athena started to speak but thankfully thought better of it. She remained silent as I continued.

"I am helpless. I will never again feel safe. I was not safe with suitors. I was not safe as a priestess. I was not even safe within your sacred temple. I don't want to live this way. People will look with only pity or disgust now. I have been looked at enough for a thousand lifetimes. I don't want anyone to ever look upon my face again. My face has brought me nothing but pain but it is those leches who should be the ones suffering. If only I could shed this skin as a snake would, maybe then I could find peace."

Athena listened intently to every word I spoke. When my words were finally spent, she shared with me the idea that would change my fate forever. "You are my dearest friend. I ache to give you all that you are asking for. What if I could turn you into a

weapon? I could make you a tool of destruction with the power to not only keep you safe but also to punish men who would hurt women as you've been hurt. I can grant you the revenge you deserve."

I took a deep breath and slowly blew it out with the little strength I had left. "I told you, I will not have a war begun for my sake. It is always the women and children who end up suffering the most for the men's pride in war. Please, Athena. No."

"I agree with you, Medusa. Declaring open war would be stupid. Rushing to fight would mean I am as irrational and blinded by emotions as a man. No, my suggestion is very different. I could strip you of your natural born form that has tortured you for so long. Your image, just your name will strike fear in the hearts of even the bravest men. Within you I will invest the power of instant death over any man."

I looked at the floor and shook my head. "Athena, I know you want to help me. Thank you. But giving a woman like me such power will anger the gods and encourage their wrath. It is no different than declaring war."

"Not if we allow them to believe I have cursed you with this new form as a punishment for the sacrilege that has happened in my temple." Now her voice had risen in fury and righteousness. It echoed off the temple walls as she roared, "You say you wish to shed your skin like a snake? I believe you. Let's do exactly that! We shall give you the body of a powerful serpent more terrifying than the world has ever seen. Not an inch of your body will be left exposed for them to violate. Even the hair on your head will be as petrifying as a writhing nest of snakes!"

I tried to envision it and wondered if I could really live that way. It would be an existence unlike anything I had ever known. The thought of watching the faces full of lust I'd always been subjected to turn into faces of terror was intoxicating.

Athena was truly worked up into a frenzy now. She was pacing back and forth in front of me, like a restless predator. Her breath grew ragged as she continued.

"PETRIFYING! Yes, exactly! That's it!" Now we had come to the pinnacle of her scheme. She took a wide stance as her arm shot out, pointing at me. "I will no longer allow you to be subjected to their judgmental stares. I will give your eyes the power to turn them to stone if they dare face you. See how much damage they can do as a statue."

A silence settled over the room as we allowed the enormity of Athena's idea to sink in. I did see one flaw in her design and had to address it.

"I do see how the gods will likely believe you have cursed me. Taking my beauty and making it so no man can touch me could only be seen by them as a punishment. Overall, men cannot imagine a woman aspiring to anything other than physical beauty and pleasing them. They will believe I could never be happy without either. It will be a simple trick in that respect. However, I can't imagine what reason they would believe you have for cursing me. It was Poseidon who committed blasphemy in your temple. He is the one who defiled your priestess. I was the one attacked, helpless to stop him. How can we convince them that I am the one you chose to turn your anger and vengeance against?"

Athena's eyes locked onto mine as a knowing smile slowly spread over her face. She took a deep breath before speaking a simple truth. "Ah, but haven't you learned yet? The woman is always blamed for the man's crimes against her."

Then I heard a sound I was certain I would never hear again after Poseidon's assault. I heard the sound of my own laughter.

The sound still echoes in my head all these years later. My days have once again become mundane and quiet. But now they are occasionally interrupted by the nuisance of a man looking to prove his bravery in conquering the feared Medusa.

Some of these men have been inspired to come here by their own egos. Many have been sent by Athena once she feels they would serve the world better as stone decorations. She trained me well in battle and turned me into an excellent weapon of justice.

My statue collection grows and litters my land with forms that used to be men. Each one I add makes the world a safer place for women. Each stone I create fills a little more of the fracture within me.

I will not be the one to crumble.

Terrible Truths

by Linda D. Addison

Part of an ancient triad of sisters, not the first,
  but the most memorable, my true story
  concealed behind myths of bitter men.

Frozen with fear by my strength, my rejection
  of their savage desires, called monster,
  declaring my power to turn flesh to stone.

To satisfy failure to control, a lie severs my head,
  sculpting me with mouth open, silent scream
  a cautionary tale to all sisters to be agreeable.

Reborn with each generation, their need to control,
  even as my twisted image remains, awakening
  the release of fury from new sisters' mouths.

Even now they avoid our eyes, afraid of hearing truths
  no longer suppressed, their base cravings denied,
  our mouths open, dreaded snakes waiting to strike …

Ghosted

by SJ Townend

Poseidon@Medsss: I'm out. Walked right out. Bunch of spanners, the lot of them except for Bacchus, he was okay in small doses. Ares did my head in, always picking fights, such a wannabe alpha-male. Even Zeus started to grate. I'm absolutely rushing right now. It's brilliant being free. Still in Majorca but they've put me up in a hotel away from the main Love Island villa. Can't believe I wasted three weeks of my life like that, Meds. Can't believe it's been a year since we split. *sadface emoji*

Poseidon@Medsss: I'm sorry, I should've said—Athena gave me your new number. Hope you don't mind me messaging you? Guess it might be late where you are. Are you still living out in the caverns of Hespirides or did you make the move to Libya? Heard you were eyeing up a run-down traditional pit house in Tripoli; a doer upper? Wasn't gossiping, just overheard. News travels fast amongst the Gods I guess. XXX

Poseidon@Medsss: This is the right number. I double checked. Iphecles knows it's live for sure, you've been chatting with her this week from it. Athena told me so. Why won't you answer me? Meds. Please. I want to talk with you.

Medsss@Poseidon: ...

Medsss@Poseidon: ...

Poseidon@Medsss: I get it. You're still cross. I understand. Thought it was what I wanted: the supermodel thing, the perfect girl on my arm. Don't get me wrong, I can't lie and say I wasn't tempted in the villa. Some of the goddesses were smoking hot … but they weren't you. I miss you, Meds.

Poseidon@Medsss: Meds, love. It's been 24 hours since I last messaged you. Why won't you answer? I've learnt so much about myself over the past three weeks. I'm a changed God. Promise. I'm ready now. Ready to settle down, become a husband, a father, a Gorgon-lover. I don't care about how you look, how tangled your snakes are in the morning, the way your skin folds far more than it should for your years. The girls back there, in the villa, they were all tens—elevens maybe, especially Amphitrite, one hundred percent, but none of those bimbos could hold a conversation like you. Those goddesses read nothing but trashy magazines and they weren't interested in history, politics, culture, science, the arts. Couldn't even cook for themselves. I had to bring in fresh fish from the ocean each morning so we all didn't damn near starve. They certainly wouldn't have adapted to a curse the way you did. I see now, how you nurture your affliction, how you care for each and every one of those hissy reptiles which spring from your scalp. You treat them with the same love, offer them the same safety, compassion, and words of wisdom you offer our son. Don't think I've forgotten about him either. I send him a birthday card every year. I'm a good father. Last night, I fell asleep thinking about you, about how your strength and love and conviction pulled Pegasus through his darkest moment, when he realised he was not like the other horses. You taught him to see his mutation as a gift. I recall clearly how, in response to your reassurance, he opened out his wings for the first time and took flight, and with a broad smile and a new twinkle in his eye, he soared above us both. I've realised, my love. I've realised what we had. What we have. We've something truly beautiful. I don't care if I can't ever look at you again. I want to be near you, with you.

Medsss@Poseidon: …

Medsss@Poseidon: …

Poseidon@Medsss: I see you there! I see those three dots flickering up on my screen. Please Meds, answer me, tell me you feel the same way. Physical beauty is no longer my priority. I know now I see you not as perfection for something as temporary as your appearance; but for what you hold within. Within, you contain something more precious than flawless skin, shiny bouncy curls, come-to-bed eyes, or a figure like an hourglass. You have a beautiful soul.

Poseidon@Medsss: Still no response? You've left me no choice. I need you so bad, want you so bad. I'm DM'ing Lamia. See if she can't help us with our 'logistical issue'. Must surely be the reason you're ignoring me: the logistics of your silly curse. You're concerned. I know you Meds—you don't want me returning for fear I'll not be able to help myself but look at you. And you love me so much—you must do, I remember how things used to be between us—you're worried I'll join the others, become a human stalagmite in your garden, wherever that may be.

Medsss@Poseidon: …

Poseidon@Medsss: You understand my plan, don't you? It's the only way. Don't try and stop me. I'll do what needs to be done, whatever it takes, and then I'll come to you, my darling. Can't wait for you to take me in your arms again, for you to touch me with your fingertips, whisper sweet nothings in my ear, kiss me in my darkness. XXX

Poseidon@Lamia: <text-to-speech> Lams, mate. Help a brother out. It's Meds. She won't return my calls. Doesn't want me getting hurt I guess, what with her condition. But I miss her. Want things to be how they were, back in the day. You remember the good times, don't you? How happy I was, she was. I think she was. Never said she wasn't. I need to come over. Today. Do you still have the sharp spoon?

Lamia@Poseidon: <speech-to-text> Dude, you've lost it. You sure this is the way to go? I haven't heard from Meds in a long time, mate. Maybe she just wants some space? Maybe she's happy the way things are? Some people like their own company.

Poseidon@Lamia: <text-to-speech> Nah, I know her mind better than she does. She misses me. Did you see me on Love Island? How could she not want a piece of this bronzed Adonis. <selfie> <selfie> <selfie> <selfie> <selfie> <selfie>

Lamia@Poseidon: <speech-to-text> Dude. Seriously. You really are all brawn, no brain. I have no eyes, bro. Can't see the selfie you sent even if I wanted to. The six selfies you just sent. Come on over though, if you like. And yes, I've a range of sharp spoons.

Poseidon@Medsss: <voice note> I've done it. I thought the bleeding and the agony would never end, but I've done it and the pain is settling now. The ambrosia and the mead are helping, taking the edge off. They're gone. Lamia works wonders with her set of rusty cutlery. Both of my ocean-blue peepers are gone. Guess no-one will be losing themselves in my deep lagoons anymore. But now there's no risk; no chance of your affliction solidifying me. We can be together now, Meds, together forever. I'll fetch some nectar and be with you before sunset if I can. And Bacchus is out of the villa now too, he came over yesterday. I told him all about us getting back together. He said he's over the moon, said it's a good reason to party. He's gifted us a case of celebratory wine, I'll bring it along. Just tell me where you are, where I can find you.

Medsss@Poseidon: YOU ARE BLOCKED FROM FOLLOWING '@MEDSSS'.

Quiet Life

by Christina Sng

Mama kept me safe
Since the day I was born.

We lived in peace,
In the heart of the forest

Till the day
The hunters arrived.

They spied our cottage
Through the thick foliage

And cut through it,
Trampling all over

Our vegetable garden,
Scattering our chickens.

Mama stormed out,
Shotgun raised,

Told them to leave
Right away.

They refused,
Shooting her till she fell,

Before they trespassed
Into our home

With their filthy boots
And bad cologne smells.

I emerged,
Silver eyes glinting

The snakes on my head
Angrily hissing,

Our eyes glaring at them
As they screamed,

Watching their flesh
Swiftly turn into stone.

I ran to Mama,
Clasped her in my arms,

Leaned forward
And let my snakes

Clamp their jaws
Onto her wounds

To siphon away
All the poisonous lead

From her battered,
Bullet-ridden body.

In moments,
Mama woke up healed.

Her eyes glinted silver,
Like mine,

And now,
Like mine,

Her newly-grown snakes
Flailed with fury.

We dragged the statues
Onto the perimeter

And lined them up there
Like sentinels.

"Would you ever want
To go back to civilization?"

I asked Mama that night.
She looked thoughtful.

"I might …
With you by my side."

Our eyes lit up
The night sky.

Sledgehammer

by Ann Wuehler

The Sledgehammer Agency nestled between Graywolf's Guns, Gold and Pawn, and Slow Betty's Bar-B-Q Wholesale Supply on East Flamingo. Teresa Ruiz tugged her niece toward the bright lemon-yellow door. Crissy followed that wide familiar back into the narrow front office, where the roundest woman she had ever witnessed sat scribbling longhand into a notebook while seated at a folding table. Not fat, but round, with a round face, a round solid body, rounded arms that would feel soft and firm wrapped around you in a bear hug.

The fake pine-paneled walls held watercolors of snakes, in mostly blue, gold and green smeary attempts. A closed bright purple door that probably led to the bathroom, to any other offices. The backside of the yellow door held a mural depicting a woman either making out with a large red-orange serpent or fighting it with her bare hands. Crissy could not quite decide. A smell of patchouli, lavender and tea tree oil assaulted the nostrils.

Teresa sneezed.

The black head lifted, bright black eyes regarded both of the women. "You must be the aunt and niece. Expected. On time. Great. Fabulous. Just knock on the purple door. Miss Deuce might be on the phone. I have snacks if you want anything. Corn nuts? No? Not everybody appreciates corn nuts. Just knock."

The voice had the quality of fingernails on velvet; it should make you wince but you wished this round being to speak about corn nuts for a good five minutes more. Odd, just an odd, strange voice.

Teresa threw out her fist to rap on that door, after Crissy cleared her throat and indicated her aunt do so, but it opened first.

Muddy Deuce stepped aside, her blood-red lips moving upward in greeting, the stench of coffee washing over Crissy. "Right on time, Teresa. The niece? Excellent."

She held out an elegant hand toward Crissy, who accepted it, noting the woman had a strong grip. Like her aunt. No rings or jewelry, but this shady lady did not need such distractions.

Stunning. This woman stunned the eye despite her handsome head swathed in a dull red paisley head-wrap, her eyes covered by gaudy showgirl shades, with fake rhinestones dotting the frames. A Sophia Loren-type of face, high cheekbones and all.

"You must be Crissy."

"I must be." Crissy chanced a quick look about the small office. Boring smeary landscapes, as if painted with underwater effects. A silver plaque with the Sledgehammer Agency etched across it in curly black letters, the woman's name under that. A bookcase stuffed full of pamphlets, fairy tale collections and straight up bondage porn. "Strange collection of books."

"Yes. Everyone has their tastes. See something you like?"

Crissy smiled, let her eyes drink in everything possible without being too obvious. But the dame didn't seem to care. Had Teresa told this Muddy she was a cop? "Beauty's Punishment. Just an odd thing to have in a … what sort of agency is this?"

Private investigation? Psychic? Crissy had never heard of the Sledgehammer Agency. But Las Vegas had a way of sheltering kooks and frauds. It was just too damn hot to ferret them all out. If they fleeced a few tourists and mostly followed the laws, these shady places could remain in business. Tourists ran Vegas.

"What do you do here, Miss Deuce? I'm just curious."

"Crissy!" Teresa sat, clutching her giant orange purse. "Focus on something else. It's all ready, Miss Deuce?"

"No judgment," Crissy offered, taking the only other chair for clients. They got folding chairs, the alleged assassin got a cushioned office chair behind a tidy white desk that held a notebook, a jar full of pens and pencils and a laptop. "Did I mention what I do for a living?"

"Crissy! Stop it." Her aunt huffed and snorted, as if the law meant nothing at all here. "I'd love some coffee. Coffee, Crissy? We'd love some coffee."

Muddy walked over to the French press, poured three cups of coffee into delicate daffodil yellow cups. No cream or sugar in sight, but Crissy could drink coffee any which way. Muddy set the two cups before Crissy and her aunt, walked around the desk to sit once again.

"Thanks. Now. What services do you offer? Tarot? Murder for hire? Dead pets from beyond the grave? BBQ tips? Buying desert acres for a survival bunker?"

"It will help you. I brought you here to help you." Teresa slurped some coffee, made a face at the strong brew. "You never let anyone help you."

"You know better than this, Aunty." Crissy tasted the coffee. Strong enough to melt her teeth. She and the fraud sitting behind the white desk shared coffee preferences.

"I enjoy your caution, Crissy, was it? So far, we're just talking. No money has changed hands. I don't collect until the dust settles."

Something twitched beneath that head-covering. The press of something long and cylindrical clearly seen against the cloth. Muddy patted that bulge back into place.

"My aunt hasn't paid you any money? You've met, what, three times, four times? Yet, no money, no retainer. What gives? That's gambling a bit much." Crissy waited, even leaning forward a bit. "Even for Vegas."

"Failed standup? Is that why you're perhaps a cop?"

Muddy grinned openly, Teresa tried not to spray coffee out of her nose, snickering away. Clearly her aunt had a bit of crush on this enigmatic charlatan. "My services are absolute. There's no undoing what I do. I give my clients every chance to back out, change their minds. Once you cross my Rubicon, that's it! You have that money order, Madam Cleves?" The voice had a low smoky quality, that whiskey voice some women had.

"Auntie." Crissy clamped her fingers on her aunt's wrist, as Teresa dug into her pumpkin-hued purse to flush her money down this fraud toilet.

Was this about the principal from Bonanza High School? Maybe Muddy Deuce billed herself as a witch, claimed she could do actual curses. People fell for that malarkey all the time.

"Fuck off," Teresa said, finding that money order, handing it over. "This is for you, Crissy. Savings account gone. Worth it."

"Don't. Or I'll haul your ass in right now, lady," Crissy warned, but Muddy Deuce took the money order, tucked it down her shirt front. As if that skinny thing wore a bra!

Crissy stood, ready to kick butt and bring the thunder down off the mountain on the thief's head.

"Crissy, no. It's for real. It's real. Vengeance, relief, peace, it's all real. Miss Deuce can deliver. I want to do this! It's my money. Mine. I earned it."

"I can't let you blow your life savings on ... Did you say vengeance?"

"David."

Crissy could not move or breathe at the sound of that name. It caused her ears to bleed, it caused her belly to turn into knots amid a sour ocean of acid. Teresa took her hands, squeezed them, let them go. Muddy Deuce sat back, her lips quirking at this domestic drama she had to witness. Something moved and squirmed beneath her head wrap. Something glittered behind the showgirl sunglasses, as if the eyes had been turned on, rather like neon signs at the coming of darkness.

"Shall we wrap things up in the basement? I will give back the money if there's a change of mind." This directed at Teresa.

Teresa faced the much taller woman. Teresa the resolute and determined tornado, leaving a roof here, taking a barn there. Teresa who had taken in her niece, while struggling to finish schooling.

Crissy trailed after the two, storing up details. That name had thrown her but she had a possible arrest to make soon. Rickety wooden steps, down to a narrow hallway, to yet another brightly painted door. A red door.

Muddy opened it and Crissy's world fell apart, shattered, refused to reform just yet.

David Ruiz, on the run now the last eighteen years, sat on a block of wood in the middle of an empty room, with nothing else there but a sledgehammer leaning against the far cement wall. A single overhead light, directly over him. A black scarf gagged him. His wrists and ankles had been bound with white rope. Not a stitch of clothing. He sat there as God had made him. Skyclad as all hell.

She had not seen her dad since the day he had beat her mother's head in with a full bottle of Jack Daniels.

She had not seen him since her Aunt Teresa had grabbed her, yanked her into the bathroom, locked the door, put her own body between Crissy and David, just in case he came for his teen daughter next. Teresa armed with a plunger and a broken shard of glass grabbed after breaking the mirror with her elbow. Blood trickling down her arm. Dripping to the bathroom floor as she waited to do battle.

Crissy had stood in the bathtub. Her mother screaming that she loved him, she loved him.

"Do it," Teresa whispered.

Muddy removed that cloth about her head. Snakes sprang forth. Living snakes that somehow grew from her skull, violet-jade snakes hissing and moving. "You sure?"

"Do it," Crissy whispered, somebody whispered for her. Her fists clenched.

Muddy lifted those shades from her face, her back to the aunt and niece, her gaze on the brother-in-law and father.

The living man turned to dead stone.

Crissy could not breathe. Shiny, light gray stone, a perfect replica of her father. How?

Teresa went for the sledgehammer. She brought this to Crissy. "Smash him, Cristina."

The weight of it. Not too heavy. She swung that sledgehammer, she heard someone screaming, crying, laughing. She heard the smack of a whiskey bottle against her mother's skull. She heard the crack of stone giving way to brute force. She got stone dust up her nose, making her sneeze.

Teresa took the sledgehammer from her numb hands, whacked at the rubble still left. Muddy Deuce had her shades back on but the snakes floated and fought each other in the dusty air. Crissy rubbed at her wet eyes but they kept leaking. Someone kept sobbing, someone kept sobbing and wanting their mom back, their sister back.

"I might be cursed, yada yada," said Muddy, leaning against the doorway. "But a girl's gotta make a living. Take all the time you need, ladies."

Tinder Ad

by Amanda Steel

Looking for someone
Who doesn't mind not looking at me
I have long hair
You must like snakes
A blind reptile lover would be perfect
Someone who doesn't mind
If I'm cold-blooded
Or the statues cluttering my house
Each of them resembles one of my exes
Purely coincidental of course
I've been alone for a while now
And looking for anything
A relationship, friendship or just some company.
And sorry, no pictures available

Gorgon's Gaze

by Ellie Detzler

The sun was warm overhead, she could feel it beating down on her skin, and she could even see the light through the cloth wrapped over her eyes. She smiled as she walked carefully down the path, tapping her cane to either side to ensure her way forward was clear.

At one corner of the path, she reached out for a statue she knew sat there. An archer, his arrow facing towards where the sun sets. She stepped around him to the right and continued on the path. The hand not holding her cane gently swept the plants on her side.

She paused to rub her fingers briefly over the petals of one, releasing a wave of aromatic scent into the air. She sniffed deeply, keen senses attuned to the world around her. The scent of lavender was powerful, heady on the wind. She smiled; perfect time to collect some petals.

She knelt down, feeling for the smaller statues that signified the limits of the lavender plot. A squirrel to the right, a bird to the left, caught in midflight, one wing broken from when it fell. She carefully cut the blooms that were the most fragrant, then when she had enough, she bundled them together to put in a basket on her arm.

With the lavender gathered she continued down the path. She ducked by memory under the spear of another statue. The spearman marked the edge of her garden—she knew without looking that his shield arm had broken off during a storm. She thought one of the kids had made off with it to use as a cauldron

45

for their games, when they mimicked their mother making herbal remedies.

She paused as the faint sound of distant bells caught her ear. Her smile widened, before she turned her face to the gravel at her feet, her eyes squeezed shut. She double checked the cloth that covered her eyes. Spending all day blind was better by far than risking any of those she loved falling under her gaze. Even the errant creature, like the bird or squirrel, was not safe from her eyes. With her blindfold secure she stepped forward to the gate of her garden as the tinkling of the bell grew louder and closer.

"Momma!"

"Mom!"

The cries of the two girls sounded as they sighted her. Rather than rush to meet them, she crouched down, her arms wide as her daughters ran to her. Like a pair of rams, they cannoned into her. She laughed, rocking back so they didn't hurt themselves, and held them both close. Even with the blindfold in place she kept her eyes tightly closed. It would only take a single misplaced jostle of the cloth for tragedy to strike.

"Oh, my darlings! I have missed you."

She pressed kisses to her daughter's cheeks. the younger one laughing as the serpents in her hair peppered her face with small kisses, the older child pretended to struggle, acting like she was too old for her mother's kisses. She released the pair of them, rising to her feet as the jingling of the bell paused only a few feet behind the girls.

"Medusa, my love," the woman's voice said fondly.

Suddenly there were arms thrown around her shoulders, kisses pressed to her cheeks, and another pressed to her lips. Medusa kissed her back just as warmly, their daughters pressing themselves between them, forming a family hug. "Euterpe." Her wife's name fell fondly from her lips. "How was the trip?"

"Oh, as droll as ever," Euterpe said, a smile in her voice. She pressed another kiss to Medusa's cheek. "I did find something there you might think is interesting."

Medusa arched an eyebrow, the serpents in her hair rising quizzically. Together the little family pulled the cart to the house, stashing their goods away before entering the cottage itself. Euterpe took off her necklace of bells that let Medusa know she was approaching and hung it next to the door.

As the kids gathered around the table, happily telling stories and chatting over each other, Euterpe pressed a small clay object into Medusa's hands. Her sensitive fingers ran over the relief stamped into the clay, her frown deepening. She recognized the monstrous visage of the gorgons. There were not many out there who had truly seen her face or that of her sisters, but there were stories aplenty of the horrors they had supposedly committed. It was distressing to know that the reliefs with this facsimile of her face had reached this close to her home. The last thing she wanted was for her children to hear one of the stories and grow to fear her.

"You know, the funniest thing happened." Euterpe's voice cut through her musing. "The merchant who had brought these had a whole collection of these clay reliefs. He said he brought them from far away, but I guess he was very clumsy for a merchant. He fell and dropped his entire basket filled with the reliefs into the path of a coming donkey. Every single one was shattered. I guess this is the only one that survived."

"Oh!" Medusa's smile widened. Then she let the clay slip between her fingers to shatter on the floor. "Oops! I guess the merchant isn't the only clumsy one!"

The two women laughed together as they picked up the broken clay pieces. The clay would join the rest of the crushed gravel on the path, where neither of them would have to worry about their children finding it.

They both knew that the world could be unkind to those it saw as different. From the scales on her neck to the snakes in her hair, she knew well that there were many who would fear her as a monster to be slain without remorse to say nothing of the power of her gaze.

Neither of them wanted their children to grow up knowing the horrors of how the world thought of their mother.

Euterpe began putting away the foodstuffs she had acquired at market. Meanwhile Medusa took charge of the children to clear away the rest of the household necessities Euterpe had picked up. She smiled as Alyssa and Thalia chattered around her about everything they had seen at the market. Apparently, the pair had played a new game with some other kids in the market that they were excited to play together now that they were home.

Medusa's smile slipped from her lips and she turned her head, a faint sound carrying on the wind to her keen ears. She ushered the kids indoors, catching her Euterpe's attention as she entered.

"We're about to have some guests," she said softly.

Euterpe ran to the door, while Alyssa grabbed Thalia and pulled her to the door of the backroom. The backroom had no windows or cracks in the door. If there was ever a danger the children knew to hide there, lest they see Medusa adding to her sculpture garden. Medusa stood slowly, one hand rising to her blindfold, but not risking touching it yet. She privately hated that her family had to be this rehearsed and practiced when it came to dealing with threats, but it was the hand the Fates had dealt her.

"Looks like it's two women," Euterpe said from her spot by the window. "One's injured."

"Ah. They have come for healing. My love, would you go welcome our guests while we prep the medical room?"

Euterpe nodded and jogged out the door.

Medusa kept an ear on the sound of her steps on the gravel outside to ensure no harm befell her. She turned to her kids. "Shall we get ready for some injured guests?"

The two girls nodded. Thalia was still too young to be of too much help, but there were some tasks that even a small set of hands could help with, such as clearing the dining room table of dishes, and with Alyssa's help putting a wide clothe over the table.

Alyssa took to the healing arts like a duck to water. Soon she would be of an age where Medusa would consider her an apprentice as well as daughter. Alyssa prepped bowls and bandages, before running out to fetch clean water from the well. Medusa heard Euterpe's voice as she finished setting up her workspace.

"… yes, my wife is the one with the medical knowledge. I'm more inclined for the musical arts rather than the healing ones," she was saying. There was a pregnant pause as they stopped outside the door. "Our children are within, so I must ask you to keep your voices down when you see my wife."

There must have been some motion of ascent as shortly the door to the house opened. Medusa turned slowly giving them time to process her appearance. One gasped, while the other muffled a shriek.

"Hera's Grace!"

"Hmm. Hera's grace indeed." Medusa smiled. "Not usually one I would invoke for healing, unless there's going to be a birth, but you can call on whomever you choose."

Medusa knew what she looked like. She knew the stories told about her and her sisters. She towered over the two women, fully head and shoulders taller than them. Her hair a nest of vipers. Scales as hard as stone ran down from her face, covering most of her body. Her wings, large and far too heavy for sustained flight arched up over her shoulders. Sharp tusks pushed out of her lower jaw, while fangs hung from the upper. If her eyes were uncovered, she knew they would be gold and blood red. Not that anyone could look upon a gorgon's gaze without turning to stone.

Whether her visage and power were blessing or curse she couldn't say. Athena's protection so she would never be raped again. Or Poseidon's wrath for spiting him. Regardless of which deity saw fit to twist her into a monster, people's first reactions to her were always one of horror. If she bared her eyes, horror would be their last emotion as well.

The only person who hadn't immediately reacted with fear upon seeing her had been Euterpe. She had stumbled upon the home Medusa had made for herself, past the stone sculptures of those who had tried to kill her like a beast. Euterpe was already very pregnant with Thalia and held young Alyssa in her arms. Medusa had cared for her wounds, treated her with kindness and for the first time felt that kindness returned. Eventually, blossoming to love as they cared for each other.

Euterpe was the one who immediately mollified the two women. She stepped past the pair, ushering Alyssa and Thalia out of the way. She gestured for the one who walked with a heavy limp to the table where she could take a seat. Thalia grabbed the hand of the other woman and pulled her to a seat and began explaining, very quickly, the importance twigs serve in a proper mud pie

"Thalia. Would you be so kind as to grab some chamomile from the garden?"

"Of course, Momma!" Thalia ran full speed out the door, leaving the other slightly baffled woman alone.

Medusa turned to the injured woman, trying to make sense of the myriad of sensory information she was receiving. Not being able to see her patient made things difficult but she had other ways to gather information. The woman stank. Layers of sweat from days of travel. The scent of blood, some fresh, some old. And beneath it all, rot. She could feel the heat of the infection in a deep laceration in her leg.

"You've come quite a way," Medusa said simply, as she helped the woman shed some of her layers. "Your leg is infected, but not so far gone that you'll lose it. Your other injuries may be superficial, but I will address them first while I prepare to treat your leg."

Alyssa stepped up to help her mother with cleaning the woman's injuries.

Medusa could hear her stifled gasp when the leg wound was uncovered. She could also hear the pounding steps of Thalia running back, no doubt with a fistful of flowers.

"My love, would you take your sister to the kitchen to make some calming tea?" she whispered to her daughter. Alyssa was more comfortable around injuries and was old enough that the sight wouldn't give her nightmares, but Thalia was still young.

"Ok, Momma. Should I use the lavender you picked this morning as well?"

"Yes, that would be perfect."

Medusa turned and pressed her nose to a bundle of herbs hanging from the ceiling, nodding in approval as she did so. She pulled them down and handed them to Euterpe. Euterpe wasn't as skilled in the ways of medicine, in fact she would soon be outclassed by her own daughter, but she knew enough to help out as Medusa's assistant while she treated the surface wounds.

Quickly, yet methodically, Medusa set about treating what she could. Her daughters prepared tea for the guests. The uninjured one, who eventually remembered to introduce herself as Berdina, took the tea with relief, hoping it would calm her nerves. She had half carried her sister, Cliantha, for miles after they were attacked by a suitor after Berdina tried to cancel their engagement. In a furious rage her suitor had attacked her, but Cliantha dove in the way, taking a blow that could have killed or crippled her sister.

Together the two of them escaped, Cliantha injured and bleeding. It took them two days to travel to where they had heard a healer lived, a healer that, it was rumored, also served as a protector for the injured under her care. Medusa was privately pleased that the rumor of a healer had traveled so far, yet had no mention of the healer's appearance.

Medusa prepared a poultice to apply to the wound that had grown infected. The mix of herbs would draw the infection out of the wound and help her body heal. It would take her a couple of days of rest to be back on her feet, but Medusa was confident that she would be back to dancing soon enough.

Eventually, Cliantha's wounds were dressed and she was wrapped in a simple chiton while she rested. Berdina was over the moon knowing that she wouldn't lose her sister. She had felt a terrible guilt that her sister was injured because of her suitor and was terrified she would lose her.

She desperately tried to press coins into Medusa's hands, but she rebuffed her.

The sun was setting outside as Euterpe invited the two to stay for dinner. Before either could respond, Medusa whipped her head around, again turning her attention to the path that lead to their home. The others froze, even the children growing still in their play.

"Riders," Medusa growled.

Both Berdina and Cliantha froze, looking at each other in terror.

"Keep the children in the house."

Medusa grabbed her cane and a drab robe that covered and obscured her features. Throwing the robe on, she hunched her body forward so that with her cane she looked like she could be an old blind man. She stepped out of the house, closing the door tightly behind her.

She strode forward on the gravel path in front of her house, using her cane to find her way to the gate. By her count there were three riders, though it was always harder to tell with hooves. They pulled up to a stop just a few feet from the gate.

"Old man, we are looking for two women. One of them is to be my betrothed. Have you seen a woman named Berdina? Her sister kidnapped her to prevent our marriage."

Medusa snorted, but didn't otherwise respond. Berdina certainly had a very different view of their supposed wedding. Men like this always thought they could take whatever they wanted.

"Well? Speak up, old man! Or are you dumb as well as blind!"

She stayed silent. The horses were growing restless.

"Well, I'll find out if you're hiding her one way or another."

One of the horses leapt forward, Medusa turned away at the last moment as a club shattered against her wings, unable to beat her natural armor. She could hear him turn in confusion, the other two men also pulling clubs or daggers. In one movement she flung her cloak to the side, flaring her wings and unleashing an unearthly howl. The sudden noise spooked the horses into throwing their riders.

"If you think you can take what you want then take it! Tremble before my gaze and despair!"

Medusa tore the wraps from her eyes. Like molten gold, her eyes blazed in her skull. Her screaming cry echoed again. Filled this time with rage and triumph.

All three men were frozen. Petrified. Stone. Three new statues to add to the garden.

She inspected each carefully. Berdina's supposed betrothed was frozen with a snarl of rage still on his face, ruined club discarded for a short dagger. An ugly statue. She would shatter it to add to the gravel of the path.

One of the men was petrified in a less dignified position. He hadn't recovered from being thrown by his horse, and was permanently trapped trying get up off his back. Perhaps she would place him near the well so Medusa could find the bucket easier.

The last had a look of terror stuck on his face—he alone had seen his companions turn to stone in an instant before she had turned her gaze upon him. She would place him on the far border of her garden, all the better to keep future cruel men away from her family.

It looked like one of the horses had been caught by her gaze as well, which was really too bad. The other two ran free, but this one, stone mane and all, was frozen in a single moment of a gallop. She could just see it as a center piece near the well in the garden. She smiled to herself. She would send Euterpe to the beach with the girls tomorrow. Spend some time rearranging her newest pieces in the garden while she could see without worry of harming her family.

In the meantime, she pulled the robe back up off the ground. She used the hood to again carefully hide her eyes, blinding herself once more, before she returned to her wife, her beautiful daughters, and her two houseguests.

They were safe. Her children did not need to know the horrors the men had wanted to wreak on their home. Her wife could continue practicing her music in peace, and her two guests could heal without worry. Medusa smiled again. A grim smile that brightened to a more genuine one. She may look like a monster, but she knew only true monsters ever saw a gorgon's gaze.

Return to Before

by Elizabeth Davis

"Galatea, what are you doing here?" Medusa slinks in the shadows of her cave.

"I've come to become stone again." Galatea sits on one of the rocks, arranging the folds of her dress like so.

"Why would you do a thing like that?" Medusa and her snakes hiss. "Even I heard of your beauty and the man who adored you to life."

"Used to." Galatea's hand tucks a graying hair out of sight. "Stone doesn't age or make mistakes or break your heart ..." Galatea looks out, into the setting sun. "But if I smile now, I will always be smiling."

A Lullaby from the Old World

by Katherine Silva

A humming exudes from the brick wall behind the old subway tunnel, a tunnel unused for the last fifty years or so by humanity. It is my song, my tale of a time long lost in history's crags, the truth of it smoothed into a round stone by humans' disgusting need to turn everything into a neat little package for pleasurable consumption. The world remembers a story of monsters, of a hero with sculpted features, of blood-coated swords. But there were shards lost to the darkness by those who didn't wish to linger upon their terror. History tells of a man who slaughtered a mortal monster, a creature with serpents for hair who could turn anyone she looked upon to stone. History forgets about the fate of the immortal sisters of that monster.

I am the elder, who once had a name, one who held court in my blackened caves in the old Grecian isles for centuries. I am the one who chased the hero, a murderer and a coward who couldn't best the real terror of the gorgons of old, who never returned so I could exact my delicious revenge upon him: the craven worm who killed my sister as she slept and stole away like a silent shadow was Perseus. Ironically, he died from the very head he cleaved in my cave, the very head he killed others with throughout the years of his reign.

I never sought him during this time, my rage and grief having pushed me to a depth I never thought I'd go. I didn't surface until much later, until wars were struck across the land like flint, destroying empires, forcing people from one place to the next like sand shuffled across a shore.

It is a wonder how one so ferociously considered can immediately be forgotten about. We were once revered and dreaded because of the curse inflicted upon us by the gods. When Medusa was slain, the people of Greece wiped us from their memories. The dead are immortalized, as I've come to comprehend. Her name became synonymous with our kind, a creature the likes of which the modern world has never seen. They think they have, of course. Art and literature have flattered us, chosen to depict us as tempting in spite of our terror, of voluptuous beauties whose only flaws are in our slithering follicles.

We are not, in any manner, exquisite. And aside from our thin faces, the curviness of our bodies, and maybe the daintiness of our long nails, there's nothing that marks us as female.

It matters not. The world occupies itself with exterior ornamentation, with body modification, with the need to identify, categorize, and understand. I belong to the old world and in the old world, all that mattered was survival and blood: the blood of one's family and the honoring of it.

I did not choose to become this thing. It was the burden of my sister, my blood that made us into the gorgons. Some may think I should have loathed her for her transgressions, for her decision that cast its fate onto her beloved sisters, I embraced the change. Humanity imparted nothing to me other than to accept my future as a man's property: to bear his children, and keep a home. Those things did not interest me. I didn't want to live in the shadow of those who thought me mad. I was already a monster before I was cursed, before my body was reshaped to resemble my mind.

There has been supposition about where my still living sister and I ended up, for we were the *immortal* duo of our gorgon trio. I haven't seen my sister in a very, very long time. She remained on the island, nestled within the darkness of the caverns while I chose to navigate the globe. I don't think she understands the way the world has changed, nor will she ever. Some are content with ignorance, with the idea that they will remain stagnant through time, no matter how it carves and mutilates the world around them. That island may not even exist anymore. Perhaps she is lost to the sea, buried in the rocks far below, awaiting my return.

She'll be waiting a long time.

My curiosity kept me adjacent with the ever-mutating disease called humanity. Watching their strife was at times scintillating and at others, frustrating. The idea that the gods continued to spare this entire species even after the world forgot its fealty to them surprises me. But perhaps the gods themselves withered and lost their interest. It seems like no one charges into monster dens anymore on behalf of kings, rampant on proving themselves for a foolish virgin or eager for a splashing of blood, not in the literal sense anyway …

But I have not lost sight of what has kept me lurking in the confines of this city for so long, feasting on the occasional vagrant, lost tourist, or unlucky pedestrian. That impudent man-whore who assaulted my sister, Medusa, who took her beloved head and conquered kingdoms with it, all without a shred of regret; his ancestral family lives somewhere close. I will never forget his scent. I have stored it in my memory so that it springs to mind as quickly as the scent of rotting flesh and of fresh volcanic ash.

The kin are millennia apart. The current abominations don't even know from whom they are descended. It only makes the irony of what I will unleash upon them that much sweeter. I have waited while the world has burned and grown and burned again. My revenge will be a complete and utter shock. I want them to feel the senselessness of it, as I did when my sister was slain. I want them terrified by the momentary sight of my hideous figure. I want them frightened by my vermillion tendrils as they writhe and snap and bury their fangs in tender, unprotected flesh.

Over hundreds of years, the man-whore's line spread and tainted other blameless families. It's a wonder I don't sack the entire city. There would be innocent casualties, but I care little, if at all.

Once I've finished, I will return to my sister, wherever she is. But the day I kill the last of Perseus's descendants lies far in the future. They will continue to procreate; new generations will be born for me to slaughter. Let them. It wouldn't upset me to do this till the end of time. Immortality with a purpose is a godsend. Surely the gods made me this way because they knew my destiny.

Hunger

by Megan Baffoe

I was married to my Perseus. He would have slain me, but I struck first. I hacked him apart for the sins of men.

Lust, anger, pride; my villainies are a hero's laurels. I gave up the manor and the palace. The streets are my caves. Cold. Cruel. *Free.* The first night I spent in a department shop door was the first coil in my crown of serpents. When people see me, they avert their eyes as if I could turn them to stone.

To be a woman deprived is to be the witch and the monster; hunger makes gorgons of us.

Gods and Other Monsters

by Rachel Horak Dempsey

My lawyer wants me to lie, pretend I'm sorry so they'll let me out sooner, but why should I regret saving someone? That girl would be dead, instead of just ugly, if I hadn't taken the knife.

See, my lawyer, Sheila, believes what everybody else does, that I sliced up that girl for screwing my boyfriend. Why else would the valedictorian do something so crazy stupid? It's hard to be wise in the fever of war.

It was my graduation party, my place. At least a dozen people saw Marinus take the girl into my pool house. And probably twice that many watched me go in after them.

If you believe high school gossip, no less than a hundred people saw me come out, tarred in blood. Feathered in hair.

I got into NYU, early decision. Who'd have thought I'd wind up here instead? Shelia can stuff her plea bargain crap; I'll never lie. I didn't want to hurt that girl. Marinus brought the knife into the pool house, not me. He had it against her throat, so she wouldn't scream. Makes me sick to think what might have happened, if I hadn't followed them, hadn't jumped on his back while he fumbled with his zipper, hadn't grabbed the knife.

Why didn't I cut him instead? That's the question they all ask. Well, not all, only the ones who don't know Marinus, who've never seen him.

He was the captain of the swim team. The prom king. Drives a Porsche. He's a god.

I thought I was too, I guess. When that girl looked up at me from the tiles, hair plastered to her skin with tears, I felt powerful.

The bottomless fear in her eyes spiked my blood like a line of stardust. In a blink, the whole world sharpened into focus. The blade, so light in my hand, slid through her skin as smoothly as a snake through water.

Here's the part no one ever believes. She didn't flinch. Didn't fight. The terror on her face simply smelted into rage.

I carved deep grooves in her cheeks, forehead and chin. When she sat up, I sawed hanks of hair from her scalp. Blood dripped from her chin and my fingers. I gagged on the tang of rust mixed with chlorine. Plus urine. In the corner, Marinus stood watching, motionless except for the spread of piss down his pant leg.

He got into Stanford. Not because he's particularly smart, I'll be the first to admit. In any case, last I heard, Marinus never made it that far north. His parents visit him once a month at the most expensive psychiatric hospital in Orange County. I suppose you could say I got the worst of it, but at least he got something he deserved for once. It helps a little to imagine him frozen in his bed, waiting for an orderly to change his soiled sheets.

Here's the other thing no one buys. That girl. She came to visit me. Face all sewn up with shiny pink scars like a hideous doll. It must have hurt to smile, but how her skin stretched, how her teeth flashed, when she saw me behind the glass.

We sat like that for the entire twenty minutes, staring. I wonder what she saw, while I studied the bare patches on her skull. Long, slinky coils of hair, like serpents, hung between the bald spots.

She's horrifying, but she isn't the monster.

If you think I am, you haven't been listening. I could've attacked Marinus instead, but then we'd probably both be dead, me and that girl. And he still would've gotten away with it, somehow. Gods always do.

I won't lie, so I've got five years left to serve. If that girl comes back, I'm going to ask her to visit Marinus for me. I bet that will make her smile.

She knows the truth. That's enough for me.

BOOK II

Snakehair

by Romy Tara Wenzel

I never liked the sea.

Even when my legs were long enough to wade out and pick limpets and barnacles from the sea-stacks, the dark, changeable shapes in the water scared me. They evoked the blood-tales of my ancestors, hunted to extinction by those they would name Heroes. I saw them impaled and mutilated in the drifts of seaweed and slick torpedoes of fish. The mottled waves pushed forward again and again, crashing on the beach with a terrible and inevitable doom.

Sometimes, beyond the noise of the laughing gulls and the whiskered terns, I heard a voice in the water. A liquid voice, strange and stormy. My sisters' warnings flooded through me, and I turned on my heel and ran back to our cave. Later that night, when I tried to recall the sound of that drowned voice to describe it to my sisters, all I could remember was the roar of the waves.

"You must stay away from the ocean, or a sailor will carry you off," Stheno warned, throwing a handful of mushrooms into the pot on the coals. Her vipers waved above her head as they caught scent of the steaming soup.

Euryale nodded as she pulled a tangle from my hair, and tucked a golden lock behind my ear. "Those salty sea-pirates would devour a prize like you, sister."

"I can run faster than any sailor," I said. "No man will catch me."

"He'd catch you by those beautiful tresses and take your flower before you left the sand." Stheno's vipers turned to me, onyx eyes glinting in the fireglow. "Euryale and I bear the legacy of our parents, but men will always seek to rescue you, Medusa."

I sat up from the warmth of the fire, feeling the play of light and shadow on my face. "Rescue me from what?"

"From us," Stheno answered, her mouth curved in a sad smile. "Men always want to rescue the beautiful maiden from the monsters. They can only see our ugliness."

"I think your hatchlings are beautiful," I said, putting my hand by Euryale's head, receiving a thousand kisses from their lilac tongues. "They are living expressions of what you feel."

"It is good to be seen," Stheno said, as Euryale's snakes curled around my fingers and purred. "But as a sister of monsters, you will suffer prejudice and insult. There is only one path that will protect you: you must become a priestess of Athena. If you do this, you shall be among women. No man will seek to take you from us, if you are under the goddess's protection."

"I would like that," I said. Stheno poured the soup into clay bowls.

"Then we must send you to Athens. If accepted, you will live with the priestesses to help weave the peplos for the Panathenaea."

I jerked my head up and heard the comb rip my hair. "Could you not come with me?"

"We'd be stoned to death, and our heads cut from our bodies as trophies," said Stheno, emotionless.

I was quiet for a time, as Euryale braided my smooth hair into a crown. "Your blood runs in my veins," I said, finally. "I am proud to be your sister. I will not hide my origins to climb the polis ranks."

"The gods will decide, one way or the other," Stheno said. "The old tales tell us Athena is the most just and fair of the gods. If the stories are true, she will aid you in your quest."

The magistrate refused my application. Of course he did. But a servant, staggering under the weight of a basket, took the stairs as I turned to go. As we passed each other I gave a cry of recognition. I let my hand fall on the servants's arm, and drew a viper from the box. It circled my wrist like a bracelet, and I drew out another. The second put out its tongue to taste the fine hairs on my arm. I forgot where I was for a moment, losing myself to this vivid reconnection with my sisters after days at sea.

The magistrate stood up, looking dazed, and made his way down the steps until he was my height. His eyes were strange, clouded. He half extended a hand towards the snakes, and the one around my wrist snapped at him.

"Be careful, Archon," the servant said, bowing his head. "These are sacred protectors for the temple of Athena. They are not venomous, but will bite if provoked."

"Last night I dreamed of a priestess, wrapped in snakes," the magistrate said, his fingers still extended as if in trance. "She wove a cloth so rich with mythos it changed our stories."

Dreams were sent by the gods. So it was that a sister of monsters spent nine months in the sacred villa of the priestesses, weaving the peplos for the Panathenaea.

On the dawn of the Panathenaea, we assembled at the Dipylon gate. I was proud to follow the *kanephoros*, a virgin of twelve in a full-length mantle, wearing a necklace of dried figs and carrying the first fruits of the season. Behind her walked the priestesses, old men with olive branches, and women with water-jugs. Then the sacrificial animals: she-goats, rams, bulls, and bleating sheep decorated with garlands of flowers.

If you could see me, sisters! I thought, carrying the sacred lamp into the Acropolis as an honorary Athenean citizen. When we came together to sing at the Erechtheum, the small self I had known dissolved into something deciduous, sensual, larger than myself. I felt my sisters, the island beasts, even the sea swell to sing ourselves together, as one.

I placed the sacred lamp before the statue of Athena, and we wrapped her in the saffron-dyed peplos. The procession moved outside, but I lingered to pray for my sisters at the wooden effigy. I stayed until the sounds of celebrating had dissolved, lost to the winds catching in the sacred olive tree outside. I heard water, although we were a long way from the sea.

The lamp flame flickered. I felt a sudden chill in the room, beyond the chill of the stone. The tingling smell of salt filled my nose, so strong it stung my eyes. I turned around.

His hair gleamed like kelp, his eyes pebble-black, his mouth cruel and smiling. His feet and legs were naked, the hair thickening towards the seaweed-draped pubis. Wet footprints behind him darkened the stones of the temple.

He moved towards me, the muscles under his skin tensing and alive in a way unimaginable in his statue. He slipped a hand through the pins in my hair, until it fell loose around my shoulders, scattering gold dust to the air. My crown of leaves fell on the floor.

"I remember this hair," he said. "It belonged to the girl on the island. You ran away when I called you. You could have lived in my undersea palace and had dresses woven of pearls and aquamarine, but you chose your sisters—the monsters." He twisted a lock between his fingers and ran his long fingers through my hair, snagging it at the ends. His nails were long and shining, like scales. His eyes dropped, and traced the curves of my tunic. "You have a beautiful body, now. A woman's body."

"This body is committed to Athena." *Pallas Athena,* I willed her. *If ever you were to reveal yourself to me, do so now.*

"But you are not a priestess yet," Poseidon said. "What a waste, to give this body to a virgin!"

"My body and my devotions belong to her alone."

His lip snarled at her name. "There are twelve gods of Olympus. She cannot stake claims."

"I would rather drown than belong to you," I said, tearing myself from his arms. His eyes flashed from blue to green.

"Everything belongs to me," he said. "That is what it means to be a god."

I felt the waters in me rising, commanding me to him. When I resisted, I felt them being drawn through my skin, indivisible from the sea god as a tide coming in. The very water in my organs and the salt in my blood drew me towards him, my juices flowing against my will, unidirectional and intent on my undoing.

I fought them, stumbling back, knocking the golden lamp before Athena. The flame flickered. I took the lamp and threw it at him, hoping the burning oil would catch on his clothes, in his long hair. The oil exploded in the air. Droplets of it fell on my arms, searing the skin. But a man made of water had no fear of fire, and the flames died down and went out.

She watched me, one hand on her peplos, as a snake wound around her ankles, tasting her with its tongue. Her eyes were like his, hard and black. *I wonder if all the gods have eyes like that, powerful and unfeeling. They are gods, perhaps they can choose not to feel.* I would have done so myself, in that moment. But Athena drew closer, and her brows were low and dark, her mouth tightly weft as her peplos. *Is she angry? Perhaps she comes to punish me. I have desecrated her temple.* I held my arm up to shield my face as she drew her spear, but it clattered to the ground and she clutched my hand.

"My child," she said. Her voice had shadows in it, like the sweet hissing of my sisters. "My child. I am so sorry."

I looked up, and her eyes were not *exactly* like Poseidon's, they were black, shifting to brown, and long-lashed as a doe's.

"Why did you not come when I called?" I whispered.

"I heard your calls," she admitted. She gripped my hand tighter. "My father has forbidden me to fight my brothers and sisters."

"Your father sanctioned the rape of your people. You could not protect me in your own temple." When I looked up, her eyes were blazing with fury again, and suddenly I realised: her fury was not for me.

"I am sorry, Medusa," she repeated.

The goddess held me. Her arms were reassuring, like Stheno's, and I nestled into the folds of her tunic and wept. She picked me up, and I was so tired that my head lay limp on the arm that supported me, putting my ear by the warm muscle there, blinking through the thick tears to see the columns and frescoes pass by. We went outside where a lone priest was cooking down the long bones from the feast to make colourless smoke that made the shapes of whales and sea monsters in the dim light.

Athena slept next to me, our heads on golden pillows. In the morning, we bathed in milk-water, but when I went to put on my dress of the day before, I shuddered to even look at it. Athena screwed it up and threw it in the fire, and took another out of a chest at the end of the bed.

"Put on this dress, it will suit you. And do your hair before coming down, you'll feel better," Athena said, and left me alone.

I picked up the silk dress, and buried my face into it. It smelled like her, like olives and sun, and slipped over me like a new skin. I fastened the fine belt, fashioned in the shape of a snake, and clipped the head into the tail.

I looked in the copper mirror, and my eyes tripped away, unwilling to meet the reflection. I turned to the loom instead, my fingers tripping over the weft and weave of the spun threads. On the breast beam next to the shuttle was a pair of shears. I fingered the blades, taking solace in the cold presence of them, and slipped my fingers through the metal loops.

I took the shears to the mirror, and feeling armed, met my own gaze. I barely recognised myself. My eyes were sunken and hollow, my skin blotched from crying. I looked closer, trying to see the emotion behind the eyes, as I had seen it in Athena. Who was this girl? She was vulnerable, desirable. Weak. I looked at my hair and hated it, remembering how Poseidon had wrapped it around his fingers. I twisted it back, feeling threads of it tear at the roots, and in a few brutal snips, let it fall to the floor.

The anger helped take away the fear. It snaked inside me when I thought of Poseidon, when I thought of all the men that took what they wanted.

I had not been the first casualty of war, only another no-name in a long line of forgotten victims.

"I would stay here with you always, Athena," I said, over dinner that appeared before we came down the stairs, as if set by fairies. "Can we not be companions? I can cook, and clean, and weave; I can keep your house, and keep you company when you wish."

"I cannot stay with you forever, Medusa," Athena said, although her eyes were soft and kind. I did not know how I had ever thought them to be like his, they were so warm and brown when they looked at me, now. "But I will not leave you defenceless," she added, quietly observing my face. "I owe you that, at the least. But I wish you to return to your sisters. Your sisters are not vulnerable to the whims of men. Your sisters would not have suffered what you have here, I think?"

"No," I agreed. "They are not considered desirable, and if they were, they would employ their teeth and talons. Were I blessed with their gifts," I added, bitterly. "They always thought I was the lucky one, but I see how blessed they were, now."

"I cannot defend you against gods," she said, and she pushed out her chair, suddenly, squealing the timber against the flagstones. She stood and walked over to me, offering her hands. "But I can protect you, if you wish it. You will give up your beauty, Medusa, at least the beauty that men see. Are you willing to pay that price?"

I thought of Poseidon and his salty hands. "It is no price, but a gift," I concluded.

"Then you will be my priestess, Medusa, virgin or not," she said, and flicked her tongue over her lips. "You will always be beautiful to me, to your sisters. Not all women will see you, but the ones who matter will honour you, sister."

She began to sing to me. At least, the only way I know how to describe it is singing. The sounds that she made came from crevices and hidden valleys in her throat that were long forgotten by our language, by mortal bodies. The sounds did not arrive like words at all, but landed like feathers or leaves, the creak of things growing, changing.

And yet, I recognised the sounds. The forest on my island home had whispered like that sometimes, in a language of green and shade, between seasons. It was the sound the forest made in its transitions, as the leaves fell, when the snows came, as the buds broke. It was a secret of transformation men did not have, nor women, either. Only wild things had it, and gods.

Suddenly, my throat tightened, as if an invisible hand clutched it. I closed my eyes, surrendering to her. And then more hands clutched at my breast, my organs, and I felt a great emptying, as if the rotten feeling, the fear, the horror, the disgust were flowing out of me like sea-water. They burned away like the sacred fire of the Erechtheion lamp, the flame dancing in my eyes that grew bright and hot in their sockets. My hair snaked from my shoulders, lengthening down my back, slithering along my spine and finally pooling at my feet, falling away as new, rippling things took root in my scalp and hissed in my ears. I shut my eyes: I was afraid. The growth was too sudden, too vicious.

But then I felt myself move, and I moved differently. Animal. Predator.

"Now," said Athena. She drew her shield over her head, loosening the leather straps, and turned its mirror to me. I looked into it, and I saw my sisters. My hair curled with ropes of life, that I remembered as far back as the womb, wet and glistening, tying me to my mother. But these cords ended in small faces, that yawned and stretched and cried out with feeling.

My eyes reflected pure light, like stars. I could see myself in them, but it was a strange self, not the earthy mortal of before. Athena watched the reflection, and then her face turned to mine.

"Men will fear you, not desire you. Take a last look at yourself before I arm you with my final gift." She held her gleaming shield up to my face, and what looked back at me was my own fury, a woman's fury. "Your rage is sacred. Look at your reflection on my shield! You will inspire fear into every man who beholds you."

"Fear is not enough," I said, feeling the sacred rage swell like the sea, grey and muscular. This was mine. "They must feel my vengeance, too."

"And so it shall be, if you wish it. You are magnificent, Gorgon," she said, admiring.

She kissed me then. She did not thrust her tongue in my mouth, as Poseidon had with his eel-tongue. She blessed me with her lips, warm as the sun, gentle, giving, brief, on each of my eyelids. When she pulled away my eyes were cool as stone.

"My gift to you, Snakehair," she whispered, speaking with the seriousness of prophecy. "Your protection."

Such Secrets, These Stones

by Stephanie M. Wytovich

You were tidal waves, riptides,
a century's worth of drownings,
an echo chamber of no against
the begging and pleading of pearls:

      your eyes an hourglass of erased
      legacies, the laughter of swordfish
      an open wound   screaming
      between my legs.

But in the reflections of snakes,
I was a body at war, the hiss
in my throat an abandoned cave,
a sleeping den of rage:

      my body bleeding, coiled
      in a garden of hate, this severing
      the beheading of trust, the prelude
      to the slit throats of gods.

Yet still I hold space for the creation
of monsters, my eyes a maiden
at the altar of vengeance, each statue
a repetitive prayer, a petition to wrath:

my fateful gaze a mirror of
consequence, my body a siphon
such secrets, these stones.

Leaving Athens Street

by Die Booth

"You're pretty."

"What did you say?"

The boy—man—leans closer. Melissa feels the warm stir of his breath against her cheek, although his voice is still only just audible above the thump of the music. "I said, you're very pretty."

"I thought that's what you said." It's not that she's not heard it before. This song is distracting. The kind of thing she's resigned to listening to, now that she's trying to fit in.

He tilts his head. Smiles, in that way guys do, like she's some enigma, ripe for solving. Melissa manages a polite smile back. She sips her beer.

"I'm Dan," the guy says.

"I know."

"Oh, damn. Does my reputation precede me?"

He's a big guy, with a big beard, and hair pulled back into a bun. Tonight, he's dressed in a too-tight t-shirt that stretches under his armpits and says 'Ride the wave' above a faux-distressed print of palm trees on the front. At a glance he looks kind of like Jason Momoa, but when you get as close as Melissa is, you can see how young he really is. He looks sort of nervous. Fear and desire. Melissa's smile starts to feel a little less forced.

"Yeah." She stares at him, hard. "Does mine?"

Dan's mouth twitches up at one corner. "I dunno what you're talking about."

"Right. So, you know I'm trans?" It's not like she's bothered or anything, it's just that it's nobody's business, and it gets more tedious

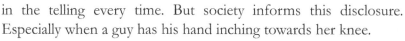

in the telling every time. But society informs this disclosure. Especially when a guy has his hand inching towards her knee.

"And?" Dan says.

Melissa's smile blooms.

"Occupied!" Someone shouts, as soon as Melissa cracks open the door.

"It's *my* room …" Then, she catches Dan's eye and they both laugh, sudden like a secret. "OK. Oh well. Let's see." She feels drunker than she should. But not in a spiked way, or anything. In a giddy way

"And whose room is this?" He follows her inside. Clicks the door shut.

"It's Tina's. She's one of my housemates. She's cool, she won't mind."

"Well, thank you Tina," he says, and their laughter this time is laced with something softer, inflammable.

Aren't all men little boys at heart? He's sweet, but she's not sorry when he doesn't leave his number. He still smiles and says hi when she passes him on the way to her Contract Law session. The lecture theatre is dozing with students. It's too close to spring break and there was the party last night … She sits in the row in front of a group of girls she recognises as Tina's friends and they fall silent, staring. The back of her neck prickles through the full hour. She thinks she might say something. Speak to them, when the lecture is finished. But then, she doesn't. The class wends out into frigid sunlight and Melissa feels strange, all the way home.

Home. The house, really. Her clothes are in the closet and her posters on the wall, but it's plainly only a stopgap. Melissa stops on the threshold, just inside the front door. The others who share the house are in the kitchen, talking. She can hear them, but can't distinguish whose voices it is of the three of them. As she gets closer to the kitchen door, she can tell it's Tina and Dita in there. They all get on alright, it's just that she's always felt a bit like an imposter around them.

"—in my room. I mean, who even *does* that?"

Melissa leans her head against the wall, silent, listening.

Dita says, "You're totally justified being upset. It's so out of order."

"I mean, it's not even about Dan, it's just about respect, you know?"

"I know."

Melissa wrinkles her nose. Braces her hand against the door. Pauses, as Tina says, "Like, I don't want to come across as the bad guy here, but people need to know, you know? People need to know what she's like. That's why I posted on the notice-board."

"They totally do. Nobody can say you're being unfair by just warning people."

A stony cold feeling of dread starts to solidify in Melissa's belly.

Tina says, "Well, now everyone will see her as the ugly person she really is."

Behind the door, Dita giggles. "Melissa? More like Medusa."

"Because she's ugly? That's so lame."

"And she's got a, y'know. Snake."

Melissa's grip solidifies on the door handle. Not stone. Steel. Her eyes burn. The giggling coming from the kitchen sounds breathless.

"You can't say that!" Tina gasps, mid-laugh.

"I mean," Dita says, "I didn't even realise Dan was bi …"

Carefully, Melissa lets go of the handle and turns and goes upstairs.

"She's just jealous," Stella says.

Melissa rolls her eyes. "Of me? Right. Yeah."

"Because Dan O'Shea is knocking down Tina's door desperate to ask her out?" says Ariel.

"Yeah, OK. Point taken." Melissa sighs. "And it's cool for me to crash at yours for a while?"

"Crash. Stay. I mean, *stay*-stay."

Melissa looks at Stella. "Are you serious?"

Ariel nods. "Hell yeah. Even just to see what she says when you tell her they can do without your rent for the rest of the year."

Their laughter, Melissa thinks, sounds quite a lot like Tina and Dita's did. She doesn't feel guilty about that at all.

"Text her now!"

"Right now?" Melissa smirks and bites her lip. Her thumb taps the glass of her phone screen. She shows them the message, *Moving out. I'm sure you'll be fine with the rent. Medusa*, and taps 'send'.

The 'typing' dots appear instantly. A reply. Stella and Ariel peer over her shoulders. *Mel, don't be like that. It was just banter.*

Melissa smiles. She taps the screen. Contact. Info. Block this caller. She slips her phone into her pocket.

"Feel any better?" Ariel asks.

"Kinda," she says.

Stella and Ariel fetch her things. Melissa feels like she dodged a bullet not having to pack. Packing is the worst. She flips open the cardboard lid of a box and stares blankly at the folded clothes inside. Black. Her old stuff, from first year. Before she learned the rules. Reality television and R 'n' B. Gossip mags and cocktail bars. It seems like no matter how hard she tries to fit in, how pretty she looks, how pleasant she is, she's always going to end up the monster. So why try? She picks up the top layer of black from the box and shakes it out. Velvet. Ruffles.

Beneath is a pile of bright green cyber falls, made of wool and mesh tubing.

"I'll give you *snakes*," she says, out loud to the little box-room.

Before she's even finished doing her hair, there's a knock on the front door. "Will someone get that?" She frowns into the little square of mirror above the fireplace, wrangling another twist of elastic around the bunch of hair in her fist. "Guys?" The knock sounds again, officious and insistent. "God's sake."

She'd almost forgotten what it feels like to walk in these boots. It's unfamiliar and comforting at once, the reclamation of a memory, the platform soles unwieldy on the narrow stairs, buckles catching against each other. When she opens the door, there's a guy there, standing on the step. She doesn't recognise him. He's practically invisible with his hood up like that: could be anybody. "Yeah?"

"Are you Melissa?" He looks her up and down, hands jammed in his pockets. He sniffs. "Yeah. You're obviously Melissa."

She crosses her arms. "And who the hell are you? Excuse me —"

The guy pulls his hood down as he pushes past her into the hallway. He's still unfamiliar.

"Percy."

His gaze darts around, not looking her in the eye. "I'm here about the rent?"

"It's been paid this month."

"Not for here." He juts his chin out. In these heels, she's a good two inches taller than him "For your room on Athens Street."

"I moved out of Athens Street."

Percy shakes his head. "Not what Tina says."

She should have seen it coming, really. The escape was too clean. Too easy.

"Oh, right. So Tina sent you to do her dirty work?"

The guy snorts. "Not even. My stepdad owns that house. It's your head if the rent's late." He looks past her, up the stairs. She hears footsteps.

"Mel? Are you OK?" Ariel asks, at the same time as Stella says, "Who's this guy?"

Melissa narrows her eyes. "He's leaving."

"Nah. Not 'till I get what I came for." His hands are out of his pockets now, fists up. He wags a finger in her face. "I've heard about you. All about you. What a piece of work you are, yeah? I can believe it. I've got on enough dirt on you on here to cut you down." He wields his phone like a sword.

Melissa feels, behind her, Stella and Ariel close ranks. Backing her up. She takes a step forward.

"I moved out of that house. I live here now. I want nothing to do with Tina anymore. She could just leave well alone, but then you come here, harassing me. Just because she's jealous of me."

"Jealous? Of you?" He laughs. It sounds nervous. "Will you just look at yourself! What do you even look like? It's frightening."

Without thinking, Melissa follows the angry flick of his hand, at the hall mirror. She sees her reflection, and she freezes. Turned to stone. She looks incredible. She looks furious and splendid and incredible.

"Get your hands off me." Her tongue is poison. Her hair coils around her. She feels like she's flying. "You think this is the same old story? Over and over again? You confront me with myself and I just lie down and die? Well, you're wrong, dickhead." She pushes him, once, in the chest, towards where Stella has the front door held open.

He stumbles towards it. He looks stunned.

"You're not the hero anymore," Melissa says, as the three of them back him out of the door. "Things are changing, and this is only the beginning."

Best Laid Plans

by Rachel Rixen

Well, that's another one wasted. I toss it over my shoulder and hear the fresh stone shatter against ancient tiles. I sigh and rebait the trap. My current success rate is only one in five and it will take nearly an entire season to catch one for each snaky strand. Determined though I am, it's rather more of a challenge than I had anticipated. Even so … they're my friends. My only friends some days, and they do deserve something nice. A fresh snack, once in a blue moon.

But, by the gods, it's hard to catch mice without looking at them!

One Stitch at a Time

by Federica Santini

there is no bridge over this personal ocean of stillness
no tremor in the head turned towards us: her eyes
draw a thin embroidery of green needles into the
ocean milk of our blood reversing its drift

steady she marks the slow tempo of change:
our hands have turned into ice eyes frozen
columns of limbs as renewed her gaze
stops on the unchanged wave

we count infinite pain
one stitch at a time

No God's Country, No Man's Land

by Thomas Joyce

The sun rose at her back, the long shadow showing the way. She used the last of her water two days ago and still did not know how many miles lay ahead. Every day she spent traversing the desert was another day he spent breathing. He had already overstayed his welcome in this world by millennia, growing fat on exaggerated tales of 'heroism'. An enforcer of the gods, retained well past his lifetime and forgotten by a father long since bored with the affairs of man.

The town appeared like a mirage at first; wooden buildings shimmering on the horizon. White and grey and brown. She had given chase over mountains, across oceans, through strange lands and stranger people. Alone. Unlike him, the conquering hero with his grandiose tales, built on pillars of sand. Mortals were blinded by the glimmer of golden-plated lies.

"You know they won't allow it."

She felt her two sisters either side of her: one vocal, one as quiet as ever. "They've washed their hands of him," she replied.

"They'll wash their hands of *you*."

She looked to the golden-haired beauty on her left, tilted her hat up to look her in the eyes. "They did that when they took her from me." They turned their gaze to the sad, silent sister. The girl with the skin as creamy as milk who had refused a god and paid dearly for it. "From *us*."

"Oh, Henny. What did you do?" asked Euryale.

She offered the ghosts no answers. Only replied by turning back to the town, her fingers slow to part from their sisters, but resigned to it.

As she passed the first outlying buildings, she noted that the town appeared the same as the last half-dozen she had visited. Undertaker. General Store. Saloon. The decomposing remains of townspeople, toddlers and elders alike, left to rot wherever they fell when death claimed them. Thousands of years spent retelling the same old stories had somehow granted him a mesmeric power. Looking upon the death this power left in its wake, she still did not know if he was unaware of the deadly result of his stories, or if he simply didn't care. It made no difference to her, or her mission.

Pausing at the batwing doors of the saloon, she listened as one voice regaled a rapt audience of past heroics, and knew, after all this time, she had found him.

She pulled her hat down low and stepped inside.

A few isolated bodies lay sprawled over different tables. They could have been passed out, drunk. But the congregation of flies over each hat or head told a different story. The live ones were assembled at the far end of the bar, crowded around her quarry.

Curly brown hair, dark tanned skin, strong jaw. Holding court like the rhapsodes of old. So full of shit.

The bartender noticed her—eventually—and brought her a shot of whiskey, but he could barely drag his attention from the hero's tales. As he was about to place the shot glass in front of her, the sharp intake of breath from the other townspeople would pull him away, and he'd take the glass with him. After his third failed attempt, she grabbed the glass with her right hand and slapped the back of his head, sending him to the dusty wooden floor. She figured she'd done him a favour; the heavy bags beneath his eyes spoke of endless days. The nearest patrons only spared her the shortest of glances before turning back to the speaker.

Most looked just as bad as the bartender, some worse. Missing teeth and rotten gums, wispy hair and open sores. The men unshaven and reeking of body odour, so too some women. Their faces gaunt, their eyes glazed over. She wondered how long they had been victims of their own veneration.

"That old fool thought he could be so easily rid of me." The hero slouched back in his over-sized seat as though it were a throne, as if he would ever be king of anything. "But I showed him. Showed his whole damned court."

"Tell us of the monster again, Lord!" The cries of encouragement which accompanied the plea were weary.

She averted her gaze, her body trembling, and noticed the bartender struggling to his feet. To her annoyance, he didn't seek an explanation from her, only to listen to this ancient story. Grabbing his arm, she demanded another drink. He poured another shot, carelessly spilling whiskey on the bar. She snatched the bottle, knowing it would never be enough. But she enjoyed the fire as it flowed down her throat. "Leave it." He didn't seek payment.

"A hideous creature," the hero began, speaking in whispers. He drank from his tankard, as though it could wash the lies from his mouth. "Born in the bowels of the underworld, a plague on innocent men whose only crime was to be fool enough to cross her path."

She closed her eyes, fought back furious tears. Recalled her sister's pain, and the unkindness done to her by their own. The only sound she could hear was the thunderous blood pounding in her veins. As it had once done in the veins of her sisters, long since dead.

"I did my duty, the honour of a victorious warrior." He stood at this, swaying, his ample gut threatening to pull him over on top of his enthralled followers.

They never moved.

"I took her head!"

The whooping and cheering that followed only ceased when she smashed the whiskey bottle on the dusty floor and roared.

"Enough of this shit." She looked sidelong at the hero and his admirers.

But only he returned her gaze. No one took notice of the golden liquid staining the floorboards.

"Welcome to my town, stranger." He raised his tankard to her. "I appreciate a woman with heart. But that was an expensive bottle of whiskey. *My* whiskey." He offered a sly grin. "But I'm sure we can work something out."

"I'm no stranger." She tried to keep her breathing steady without breaking eye contact. "You knew my sister."

"I have known many sisters in my time." He belched, looked to his followers for a reaction. But they only continued to stare.

"You *will* remember *my* sister." She gazed into the long mirror above the bar. He followed her eyes and looked at her reflection as she placed her hat on the bar. Saw her features begin to change.

The cracks spread from where his tankard connected with the mirror. "She means to kill me! Stop her!" he shouted, covering his eyes.

They moved slow, but deliberate. She only hesitated for a second; after all, it would be a mercy. In an instant, the advancing horde were frozen in place, cast ever more in their final repose.

Her hair was alive; writhing, raging for justice. Her face had twisted, contorted, her disguise cast off. The hero she sought cowered behind the frozen forms of his former followers, sword and shield in hand, eyes averted.

"How did you find me, Gorgon?"

"I have scoured every corner of this world for you." Her tongue darted from her lips as she spoke. She stalked her prey beneath the gaze of the horrific and horrified flesh statues. "But, in the end, a little owl told me."

He crawled among the grotesque monuments to his self-conceit, staring into his shield, the sword trembling. With anger or fear—or both—she couldn't tell, didn't care. "I never wanted to do it. She brought it on herself. I did her a favour!"

The venom burned at the back of her throat as she bit back tears. "She was forced to hide herself from the world. She hid herself from those who loved her!"

"She offended the gods."

"*They* have offended *me*!"

He dropped his gaze from his shield for only a moment. The snakes moved as one, aiming for the nape of his neck. But they missed their mark when he ducked, and swung around with his sword, eyes squeezed shut.

Dark blood poured from her scalp like Greek wine and covered the left side of her face, the snakes still on her head joining with her screams as she ducked behind a woman, the face frozen in a sudden and painless death. The severed snakes writhed on him, on the floor.

They slithered over his face, his body. He backed up, shaking them off, relieved to still be moving. But someone was at his back. For a brief second, he thought it was one of the frozen townspeople. His breath caught in his throat as hands covered his eyes, a forked tongue flicked his ear.

"A gift for you, from my sister."

Her sharp claws groped at his eyes, like a child digging for treasure. She resisted his flailing arms and claimed her own prize, pulling them from their sockets and crushing them in her hands. She kicked him, screaming and hysterical, into the writhing mass of snakes that had once been her hair. His wind-milling arms connected with some of the flesh statues. They fell on him, encircled him, trapped him.

"So much for heroes." She spat.

Retrieving her hat from its place on the bar, she raised a glass of whiskey to the ceiling. "For you, sister." She downed the alcohol, smashed the glass upon the floor and covered her newly short hair with her hat. Her features returned to their human form, her disguise restored beneath the shadow of the brim, the flow of blood stemmed and dried into her shaved head. Her remaining hair hid the single tear escaping her right eye. The 'great hero' of the old world endured a slow, screaming death as she pushed through the swinging doors into the heat of a new age. The new world.

Medusa. © 2022 Max Stark. All rights reserved.

The Power of Others

by L. Minton

Just like you
My first memory is of my mother
No songs or tender arms begin my tale
Only the violent chorus
Of Power abused
As her crimson blood
Emptied swiftly into sand

His very name means 'ravager'
But the murderer of my Maker
Could not even kill her!
—Not without godly intervention
Nor could he accomplish his great feats!
—Without the theft of her Power
He left kings far and wide star struck with his accomplishments
Riches, a princess, fame
Purchased only by a woman's severed head

Then plucked from wild innocence
Even before my first taste of limitless sky
Forced into golden servitude
Because the appetites of Men
for the Power of Others
Runs just as wide and just as high

Sanctuary

by Catherine McCarthy

Dussy Dracos, the sign on the fence reads, *Stone Sculptor and Snake Saviour.* Underneath, in smaller print: *Ring before entering.* A large brass bell hangs from the gate-post and a yellow warning triangle, complete with coiled serpent, is attached to the fence.

Ranger Nikolaos Kallis steps out of the truck and slams the door behind him. From the shack door, Dussy waves.

"Hey, Nik! What you got for me?" she says, coming down the path towards the truck.

He grins. "Ottoman viper, it's a beaut."

"Injured?"

"Run over, by the look of it. Poor thing's struggling, Dussy."

She tucks wild locks of hair behind her ears and watches as Nik unhooks the lid of the box. From a nearby olive grove cicadas buzz to the beat of her heart, and the bitter scent of oleander fills the air.

"I'll leave you to work your magic," Nik says, revealing the cotton sack containing the snake. No movement, not even a twitch. His face falls. "Christ, I hope it's not—"

Dussy presses a finger to her lips. "Sh, don't say it." Her right hand hovers over the fabric, close, but not touching. She makes a circular motion, slow, hypnotic, then smiles. "It's alive." She prises open the neck of the sack before reaching in, bare-handed.

"Shit, Dussy, these guys are poisonous. Use the tongs."

"No need. It knows I mean no harm." Confident. She holds the viper in both hands. Three feet long, rough-scaled and zig-zag patterned. The viper coils, then rests its head against her thumb

91

pad. "Poor baby," she says. "Let's get you fixed, hey?" The vertical slits of its pupils are milky; its tail misshapen and bloody.

Nik follows her as far as the gate.

Inside the threshold stands the stone sculpture of a naked man, reminiscent of the famous statue, *The Diadoumenos*, and just like *The Diadoumenos*, its hands are missing. No ribbon round its head though, to suggest victory. Instead, the statue's hair falls lank as it stares down at its missing hands in shock. Coiled around the stump of its left arm is a sand boa. It tastes the air with its tongue as they approach.

"You coming in?" Dussy says.

Nik shakes his head. "Too busy. Someone's been trapping goldfinches again. I need to head on over."

Her face darkens. "Assholes. Get the gate for me will you, Nik?"

He springs the latch and waits until both Dussy and snake pass through before securing it. "One day you'll explain how you manage to keep them inside the sanctuary." He gestures towards the boa, coiled round the sculpture. "I mean, they have free rein. They could escape any time they want."

She laughs and blows her fringe out of her eyes. "Ah, but they don't, do they?"

The following week, Nik stops by again. This time the rescue truck contains no serpent; instead there are sixteen caged blackcaps and a dozen goldfinches in the back. He honks the horn, alerting Dussy to his presence.

"What you got for me this time?" Around her neck she wears a smooth snake; its glossy scales shine gold in the Samos sun.

"Nothing for you, but take a look at this." The air is filled with birdsong that reaches a crescendo as she rounds the truck. "Listen … that repeated whistle, sounds like *bay-bee*." He points a finger. "Hear it? Means they're stressed."

The smooth snake stretches its head towards the birds, so Dussy unwinds it and places it inside the grounds of the enclosure. She leans towards the cage, hand to mouth in horror. "Glue?"

Nik nods and rubs the back of his neck. "Bastard. If we catch him, he'll go down for this." The songbirds bounce and flap, desperate to free themselves from the lime sticks to which they are attached, but fail to take flight. "Do you know what infuriates me most? The greed. It's bad enough that they sell them as pets on the black market, but now more and more are sold as ambelopoulia."

Dussy frowns. "What's that?"

"A delicacy. Sells for around eighty euros a bird. Sickens me, Dussy."

She shakes her head and pales. "You close to catching him?"

He taps the side of his nose. "We think he's shacked up in Platanos. Had a tip-off, but we need a warrant to search the place."

Her eyes blacken. "Platanos? Whereabouts?"

"Up in the mountains, close to the honey farm. Wooden shack, just off the track by the church." He climbs in the truck. "Anyway, I'd best be off. Get these poor things to the rescue shelter and free them from the glue." He starts the engine and hangs out the window. "By the way, how's the viper doing? Worked your magic yet?"

She nods. "He's doing fine."

"Good to hear. See you soon, Dussy."

She watches the dust billow from the ground as the rescue vehicle disappears into the distance.

Just past midnight. Dussy parks the truck at the church pull-in. In the back is a wheelbarrow and a large container, complete with air-holes, inside which a Bosnian adder lurks. She removes the wheelbarrow and lowers the adder into it. Flashlight strapped to her head, she follows the dirt-track that leads to the shack. Among the black pines, the eyes of a wild boar glow amber. She knows it will do her no harm.

From a nearby shed, the desperate cry of caged birds convinces her she's come to the right place. The shed door is locked, so she peers in at the small window, her flashlight sending the birds into a frenzy. "Hush now," she whispers. "You'll soon be free." At her words, they calm and fall silent.

She removes the adder from the sack and drapes it about her neck, then, leaving the barrow at the fence, tiptoes over and hammers on the shack door.

The poacher has no time to consider who his nighttime guest might be. The adder strikes, its target the carotid artery, and it hits a bullseye. Dussy grins as the poacher falls to the floor, clutching his neck. The flashlight picks out two puncture wounds, red and oozing venom. He clutches his throat as the swelling ensues, frothing at the mouth. Soon he is still. Dussy retrieves the barrow and bundles him in, grateful for the fact that he weighs little more than she does.

On the journey home, the adder coils atop the poacher's chest, vertical pupils fixed on his every step of the way.

The enclosure is floodlit, the moon an accessory to murder. Dussy has already chosen the spot—furthest corner of the garden, close to the mastic tree. A fitting place of rest, she thinks, considering the tree is known for its sticky resin.

On the ground, she places an empty bird cage, its door yawning open, then she strips the poacher of his sleeping shorts and arranges him in the position of the statue of *The Fallen Warrior*. In place of a shield, she props his arm against the empty cage. He remains conscious, though unable to speak or move.

From all around the sound of hissing and slithering as the den of serpents gather to watch. They writhe en masse, slithering over each other to gain a better view. "You think me cruel?" she says, eyes wild and hair a matted tangle of coils. She tuts. "There is none so cruel as those who have no concern for the creatures of this world."

She delights in the heave of his chest and the rattle of his breath. "My name is Dussy," she whispers, "short for Medusa."

He flinches at her words, the slightest twitch. His pupils are black beads. In the light of the moon, his skin is tinted blue.

"Before I turn you to stone, I must amputate your right leg at the knee, just like that of the famous statue. After all"—she gestures towards the den of serpents—"my children must eat."

When Nik shows up two days later, Dussy greets him at the gate. "You catch the poacher?"

He shakes his head. "We were too late. He did a runner the day before we got there." His eyes are downcast, fists clenched tight.

"Shame. But you set the birds free, yes?"

"Of course."

"Ah well, better luck next time." She beckons him over. "Come inside, won't you? I have a new sculpture to show you."

A Tongueless Daughter

by Ai Jiang

Your hair, like the unruly tendrils of Medusa's snakes, froze your family in place. Not that there was any magic, but because these dark threads were attached to a girl, a daughter. Your tongue is not forked, but they didn't want to see it. They told you to be silent, docile, simple. You cried but they paid no attention, and turned to your twin, the son, with love and admiration. So your hair came alive, ends sharpening, when they tossed you into the well. Your snakes shot up before you hit dark waters, dragging your brother out of their hands.

Sea Change

by Katie Young

I see the archipelago in the distance—a blurry series of humps on the flat water, like some great beast surfacing for air, shrouded in mist. My best guess is there's still at least an hour of pulling ahead of me. Maybe two. No one comes out this far. They say it's cursed—blood red pools blanketed in hush. The repetitive splash of my oars and the squeak of them grinding against the metal rowlocks are the only sounds I can hear, save for my own raspy breathing. My blistered palms throb in time with my heartbeat.

Everything aches. My shoulders, back, and forearms screaming. The sun is beating down on my exposed neck where my hair is twisted up under a bonnet. I'm pretty burnt now, but it's just one more type of pain, hardly distinguishable from the litany of hurts.

I sometimes try to imagine what it was like here in the between age—after the first great flood and before half the world drowned for good. There was a time when birds wheeled overhead constantly, diving for fish in unpolluted lakes and streams, for shrews and voles and rabbits. Animals of every size and shape imaginable roamed vast plains, mountains, and forests. Their names have been passed down through the ages. Most are gone now, but I've seen pictures in the wrinkled pages of waterlogged books salvaged from the age of libraries, before all those great cathedrals of learning were washed away, burned, or shut up by the authorities. All this would have been land back then, beautiful fields of green and gold teeming with chirping crickets and shivering with scurrying things—ants, spiders, multicoloured beetles. There would have been snakes too, slithering through the long grass, or sidewinding across mud flats and desert sands. Water snakes rippling through the seas.

I shudder, gooseflesh breaking out all over. I hope it's just the thought of those dead eyes and flickering tongues and not sunstroke. I've been rationing my water to make it last, but I stop paddling for a moment to take a long swallow from my pouch. My lips are cracked from the salt in my sweat, and in the ocean spray. The sun will be setting soon. It's already lower on the horizon, the sky darkening ahead over the cluster of islands, clouds rolling towards me.

Does she know I'm coming? Can she feel me after all these years? We were born within minutes of each other. Our mothers bonded in a grim wooden and tin building that sat on stilts like chicken legs and served as our village's postnatal ward. Mine had nearly bled to death, and hers was all torn up from a difficult breech birth. The strangest part was that neither woman's waters had broken. Both of us emerged into this world in our amniotic sacks, asleep under water, like we knew we were safer cocooned inside, hidden from the scorched and hostile world that awaited us.

Just as I could barely conceive of a time before the flood, I'd never known life without Meredith. We were like sisters. Closer. I'd find her name suddenly on my tongue moments before she'd appear in the doorway of our ramshackle little house. We shared food, clothes, and, when we were a bit older, our beds, curled up in the quiet dark, our fingers entwined, the soft brush of her skin setting off little tingles up my arm. I'd drift off with her soft curls tickling my nose and her face close to mine so could smell the sweet warmth of nettle and mint tea on her breath.

Everyone loved her, but I loved her first. I loved her best.

My hands are failing now, the skin swollen and split. The oars spin in my blood-greasy grasp, but I've come too far to turn back now. The water is becoming caustic as I near the islands, and the sea spray stings my raw flesh. There's an ammonia tang in the air which irritates my eyes and lungs. The undisturbed surface of the water ahead is glassy, a vast, dark scrying mirror until I shatter it with my paddles.

Meredith's father died at sea when we were little. I have half-memories of a man who was not my own father sitting in our house and carrying me around the village, but they are vague at best. It was hardly an infrequent occurrence in our area. People were lost to the capricious water all the time. But I suppose part of Meredith's mother was wrecked with him that day because from then on Meredith spent more time with us than at home.

One day when we were around twelve, Meredith and I were peeling vegetables for my mother. We were singing some old song we'd learnt in childhood about giving your love an apple except the apple wasn't real—the apple represented your head. The metaphor didn't make much sense to us then, but the melody was pretty and it wasn't about being judged by the gods like most of the other songs we sang. Meredith started the first line and I joined in, repeating it as she reached the second line about the house without any door, so that I followed her through the verse and she began the song again as I finished.

When we reached the final round, I sensed Meredith's gaze on me while I warbled the last line solo, self-conscious now my lonely voice was exposed. I continued to busy myself, scrubbing potatoes until the scrutiny became too much, and I turned to face her.

"What is it?"

Meredith looked down at the paring knife in her right hand, paused for a beat and then drew it across her left palm. I gasped as red welled, forming rivulets in the lines of her cupped hand.

"Are you mad?" I cried, groping for a cloth to stem the bleeding. But Meredith grabbed my wrist in her bloody fist.

"If we mix our blood, we'll be sisters. Then nothing can ever come between us. It doesn't hurt much."

And that was all it took for me to open my hand and let her make a small cut. It stung something fierce, but I didn't cry. We pressed our oozing wounds together, a hot throb spreading out from the spot where our blood mingled. I imagined I could feel my heart sucking hers into me, pushing mine into her veins, and it was done. We were bound.

The dark is closing in now, sky the colour of a bruise, and the fog is starting to envelop me. The island is close. The water here is ruddy pink, like someone bled out in it. There are markers on the approach, long poles which stick up out of the glassy surface of the water. The eerie stillness makes the fine hairs on my arms stand on end. The air smells like urine, the tang of it scratching the back of my throat, the surface of my eyes. I blink tears away and squint at the posts surrounding the largest of the islands—my destination.

They are topped with shapes I can't make out at first, but as I draw closer, I see what they are. Animals. Beasts of the air and beasts of the sea. At least they were. These are no longer living things. They are petrified. Pale husks which glow milk-white in the silvery light of the rising moon. Ghosts.

I've never seen so many species in one place. There are seabirds—a huge gull, its wings outspread, a macabre crucifixion scene. Its bones are close to what was once skin and feather, but now has the appearance of stone. There are gaps in the bird where the night shows through. Here is a bat, skeletal and hard— the veins in its fragile wings stand out in stark relief as if it were chiselled out of a marble block. There are dozens of calcified fish of all sizes, from tiny sprats which dangle from string in shoals like morbid windchimes, to a large shark impaled on a sturdy spike. My eyes stream, but I cannot look away from these wonders.

A sudden movement in my periphery distracts me from this gruesome tableau—the tiniest disturbance of the water by my boat and a ripple which spreads out from underneath it.

I recoil as a black sea snake breaks the surface, its sleek body undulating as it swims towards the island. Perhaps it has been sent to spy on me. Perhaps is destined to end up as a macabre sculpture of itself.

One day shortly after our sixteenth birthday, Meredith and I were sat on the parched soil under the scant shade of a dead ash tree, sharing a cup of lemonade, when a snake came slithering across the dusty ground. It coiled itself around Meredith's wrist. I froze when I saw it, the hypnotic, sinuous movement of its green body horribly fascinating. I'd never seen anything like it. I held my breath, waiting for Meredith to scream, but instead she slowly lifted her hand to better look at the little serpent.

"Hello," she said. "Aren't you beautiful?"

Snakes were the creature we'd been brought up to fear most. It was said that a great serpent once wrapped around the primordial egg, from which the chaotic Universe hatched, keeper of all the secrets of creation. Snakes were messengers of the Underworld, vessels of wisdom, rebirth, healing, and carnal desire. Immortality. In the beginning, humans lived in blissful ignorance, but then a time came to pass when—corrupted by knowledge and power—they learnt to prolong their natural lives, build machines infinitely more powerful than themselves and weapons that could destroy continents. They carried all of history on little devices in their pockets that allowed them to talk to each other wherever they were in the world, and transmit moving pictures so that everyone could bear witness to everything all at once, and it drove them mad. Gods could disguise themselves as snakes, and it was said a titanic, monstrous serpent was imprisoned in Tartarus, his writhing and thrashing causing eruptions of fire and magma to burst up through the mountains, along with earthquakes and tidal waves.

"Careful, Merry," I warned her, getting to my feet. "It might bite. Try and shake it off and I'll stamp it!"

Killing animals was punishable by banishment in our village, except in self-defence.

"No," she said, horrified. She looked at me then as if I were a stranger. As if we didn't know each other's every secret.

"What if it's venomous? What will I do if you die?"

"It's harmless. Besides, they only bite if you make them mad."

"How would *you* know?"

"Simeon told me he read about snakes."

My stomach lurched. Reading was forbidden in the village. Only a few elders had permission to read, and then only certain texts. Reading was knowledge and knowledge had destroyed the world more than once.

"Before the seas rose, they lived on almost every continent on Earth," Meredith said, as if she herself were reading from an unseen page. She seemed hypnotised by the serpent on her arm. "They can shed their skin, just slip out of it like taking off a dress. They are constantly renewing themselves, transforming. Reborn. They hunt by tasting the air around them and following the vibrations of the earth. They can eat things much bigger than their own heads by dislocating their jaws. But sometimes they devour themselves. Eat their own tails. Imagine that. Something in them breaks and they just ... destroy themselves."

Meredith petted the snake, and it wrapped around and around her like a bracelet. The snake stayed where it was, forked tongue scenting my friend's skin.

"It likes you," I said, fear and disgust tainting my voice. It was a little thing, but it felt portentous. There were things in Meredith's mind and in her heart that she hadn't seen fit to share with me. She wasn't afraid of snakes. She'd been spending time with a boy. A boy who could read. There was a fault line in the notion I'd always had of us and I prodded and worried at it endlessly like a chipped tooth, knowing I was tempting disaster but unable to leave it alone.

I paddle as close to the shore as I can, then leap onto the land, taking care to avoid the corrosive water. The shale here is littered with more of these unfortunates, birds and rodents and fish lying stiff and rinsed of colour as if turned to stone.

The thought of all these little lives lost is enough to make more tears needle my eyes. As I walk lightly across the beach, I see flashes of movement between rocks, and I swear I can hear rasping voices carried on the wind. Simeon was tall and freckly with hair like spun gold. He had an air of superiority which made me want to scratch his eyes out. I wanted to tell someone what Meredith had told me about the reading, but it would be my word against his and I was a girl after all. Meredith seemed to like to him, which only made me hate him more. She'd try and talk to me about him but I'd change the subject and desperately reach for something to say that would make her eyes flash the way they did when she told me about something Simeon had said.

The day I saw him in the trees with Meredith was particularly cruel and sticky. The air was viscous and smelt mildly of sulphur, as if the maws of Hell really were opening up beneath us. It took me a few seconds to understand what I was witnessing at first. Simeon's distinctive hair caught my eye first, his broad, freckled shoulders. He was standing, facing a thick tree trunk, his hands stretched up over his head, and braced on its rough surface.

I almost laughed because I thought maybe I'd caught him pissing. Why else would his shorts be down around his ankles? But then I saw the legs wrapped around his waist, the way the heels were jouncing against his flexing muscles, the dimples at the small of his back, so pale there compared to the tanned skin on the rest of his body. The smaller hands he had pinioned by his own were clutching and clawing at nothing. Her face was obscured by a curtain of hair, but I'd know her anywhere.

Meredith was silent, her body limp as Simeon hunched over her like a wild dog.

The house is more of a cave really, a stone dwelling hewn into the rock. The entrance is covered with seaweed woven into thick strands and is firelight flickering inside. My pulse is frantic now, and I swear I can feel the phantom brush of cold, reptilian scales swirling around my feet. It's cold now the sun has set, and I'm shivering although my skin is on fire. My own father was one of the men who came to search Meredith's home once word got out that she'd been communing with serpents. It frightened me how quick they were to believe there was evil in their midst.

"Help me, Althea!" she sobbed, the betrayal and accusation

shining bright in her eyes. "Tell them it's not true! You were there! You know there's no harm in it!"

My father prodded a squashed mess on the ground with the toe of his boot. A knot of ruined snakes. The sound of Meredith crying was like a knife being plunged into me repeatedly, but I couldn't think about that now. Terror seized my throat and I had to concentrate hard on not vomiting. I stayed silent.

"They'll kill me, Althea!"

I watched as the villagers gathered by the door. They pawed at Meredith as she was dragged outside, rending her dress, grabbing at her hair until it was matted and wild. They called her Witch. They accused of her performing unspeakable acts with snakes. They said she lured men into bed and bit them with fangs that descended at the height of her passion. They said Meredith had teeth down below as well, all the better to emasculate you with, nestled beneath hair that wasn't hair at all but tiny writhing snakes. Meredith could spit venom that would paralyse you.

"You're a monster, Althea," she screamed as they hog-tied her and wrestled her onto the boat. "A monster!"

I watched the commotion and listened to the inhuman sounds she made as the boat drifted further and further out to sea. I didn't understand how it was possible to feel so bad and not simply die.

I don't recognise her at first. That once lovely face is lined and pinched. She's thin and brittle-looking like the calcified creatures outside. Her long, dark hair is streaked with grey and has been twirled into thick tendrils by the wind and salt. Her eyes are milky white—unseeing pearls in her skull.

"Althea," she says, voice rough. "I've been expecting you." Meredith holds the seaweed tendrils aside and I walk into the stone house. "I've dreamt about you a lot over the years. But last night was different."

I nod, although I know she can't see me. I don't think it matters.

"You're bleeding," she says. "Are you in pain?"

"Yes," I admit. My voice is a croak.

"Good."

The place is hovel, some cursed abode from an ancient tale. Meredith busies herself by the fire, gathering bunches of dried herbs to make tea.

"You don't have long left," she says, knowing my every thought, the way she always did.

Meredith hands me a cup of pungent smelling tea and sits down cross-legged on the ground. I follow her down. Thirst gets the better of me and I gulp the herbal brew quickly, scalding my cracked lips and tongue.

"I see your heart is as calcified as those poor creatures outside."

I mean it as a joke, but Meredith is silent and I know I forfeited my right to that kind of casual intimacy when I stood by and let the villagers banish her. "I heard that you died years ago. A traveller on the mainland claimed he'd beheaded the snake-haired island witch."

Meredith sips her tea, her milky eyes boring into my soul. Her face puckers and she bares broken yellow teeth, her shoulders heaving up and down as she emits a horrible wheezing sound. I realise she's laughing.

She holds up her left hand. The silvery scar is still just about visible on her calloused palm.

"We're bound together," she says. "Nothing can come between us, remember? Not even death. I can't go without you."

I sip my tea. The isolation and wind have broken her mind completely. I shouldn't have come. Better she had died in that boat.

"That was childish stuff, Merry." That affectionate contraction rolls off my tongue so easily but it hurts on the way out. "Something did come between us."

Meredith chuckles again, but there's no real mirth in it. She sweeps her tangle of hair to one side and bares her neck. There's a ragged welt running all the way around it, like a red ribbon.

"I only hung around Simeon because he could read to me. All our lives we lived in fear of knowing the world, but what if they were wrong? What if we were lied to? There is still beauty everywhere if you know where to look. Was it so wrong of me to want to believe in that?"

"I saw you," I say bitterly. "With Simeon. In the forest. He wasn't *reading* to you then."

Meredith shakes her head and spits into the fire.

"I never wanted that," she says quietly.

Those four words knock the breath from my lungs. I can't speak, can't think around this revelation. The floor of the cave seems to shift and tilt. There's a sound like mosquitoes whining in my head. She was forced.

"I was upset … afterwards. He realised I'd tell you and you'd never let him get away with it, so he told the village I was … monstrous. They were quick to believe it too."

The tea is roiling in my stomach.

I feel sick.

All those years.

All those long years.

I can't speak.

"It doesn't matter now," Meredith says, finishing her tea. "You're fading fast and we're bound, so I will finally be able to rest."

I look at the scar on my hand.

Meredith's unseeing eyes are moist now. I realise my own face is wet with tears.

"I missed you so much," I whisper.

We sit as the fire dwindles and darkness envelopes us. The floor is cold and hard against my bones, but that feels fitting, and I imagine us turning to stone, sitting here together until we're finally eroded by the wind and water.

A Heart Turned to Stone

by Lyndsey Croal

It's hard to break a heart turned to stone. Hers is ripped from her chest, from between brittle ribs, locked away for safekeeping.

Many try to steal it—for a heart turned to stone cannot die.

She cannot die.

Now, she goes here and there, her heart a target. Her story forgotten.

If only you stopped to listen, she would tell you about her heart, help you learn its secrets.

But no one does. No one wants to hear that story. They only want the other, of the man that long ago broke her, and turned her heart to stone.

The Gift. © 2022 Elizabeth Leggett. All rights reserved.

Stone Against the Sea

by Elyse Russell

"Three hundred thousand! Going … going … gone! Sold, to Ms. Cora Aremy!"

A smile played about Cora's rose-pink lips. She had acquired her employer's desired piece of art, and at well under the budget, besides. Mrs. Harmon would be very pleased.

Cora watched as the strange box was lifted gently by one of the auction house employees. It was made of bronze, and hand-painted with exquisite detail. The scenes around the sides portrayed the cursing of Medusa: the moment when the girl had foolishly declared herself more beautiful than the goddess Athena, and her subsequent transformation to a monster.

The box was in near-perfect condition. Like the rest of the items in the sale, it had come from the private collection of one of the city's elite. Current generations were more interested in money than in holding onto precious family heirlooms. After the item was delivered to her vehicle, Cora drove conservatively to Mrs. Harmon's flat in the upscale portion of town. She was conscious of the precious, ancient Greek box in the backseat each time she had to hit the brakes or go around a corner.

It had started to rain by the time Cora reached her destination and pulled into the parking garage. She carried the box, which was far heavier than she would have thought, got into the elevator, and went straight to the top floor. At this time of night, Mrs. Harmon would undoubtedly be sitting in the conservatory.

Cora's heels clicked on the smooth tile floor as she carried the box to the open conservatory door. As she had predicted, Mrs.

Harmon sat in a plush armchair beneath the glass ceiling, looking up through the palm fronds at the pattering raindrops. She had only a single lamp on, and was listening to Mozart while sipping red wine.

Placing the box on the coffee table, Cora took the chair opposite her employer. Mrs. Harmon's gaze dropped to the wrapped piece, and she sat forward as quickly as her old bones would allow.

"Unwrap it," she croaked eagerly, her pale eyes more alive than Cora had ever seen them.

No sooner had Cora removed the protective silk cloth than Mrs. Harmon's shaky hand was running over the sides of the box, stroking it like a precious pet. Her thin lips moved as she mumbled something in the Old Tongue that Cora didn't quite catch.

Mrs. Harmon's sharp eyes darted up to hold Cora's gaze. Her tongue darted out to wet her lips.

"Do you know what this is, my dear?"

Cora simply shook her head. Mrs. Harmon preferred silence whenever possible.

"This is no mere piece of art, Cora," the old lady continued. "Unlike every other bit in the lot you saw tonight, this one was built with a very singular purpose—a sinister purpose."

Cora edged forward in her seat a bit, intrigued, her face open with questioning. Mrs. Harmon continued to stroke the box, trailing her swollen, arthritic knuckles over the image of Medusa transforming to a monster with snakes for hair.

"This," Mrs. Harmon almost whispered, making Cora lean forward to hear better, "is a prison. Tell me ... what do you know the story of Medusa?"

Cora cleared her throat. She hadn't paid much attention in history class, but everyone knew the cautionary tale of Medusa.

"She was once a beautiful maiden," she said. "She'd dedicated herself to a chaste life in the temple of Athena, but then foolishly declared she had hair more beautiful than the goddess. Then, to further cement the insult, she gave her virginity to Poseidon on the very steps of the temple. Athena was righteously furious and cursed the girl, banishing her to an island. Instead of the hair she had been so boastful of, she had snakes. And her gaze could turn men to stone, ensuring that anyone who found her in her cave would not ease her loneliness."

Mrs. Harmon snorted. Cora was fairly certain she'd never heard her employer make such an undignified noise before. After a sip of wine, the elderly woman continued.

"That is the standard tale, indeed. Very useful for cautioning girls against pridefulness and unchastity."

Mrs. Harmon leaned forward, laid her hands regally on the lid of the box, and spoke in a clear voice, in the Old Tongue. Cora struggled to understand what the old woman was saying. Children hadn't been taught the Old Tongue as well in her generation.

"I am Doris Harmon, descendant of Poseidon," the woman declared in a powerful voice.

Cora started. She'd been unaware of her employer's lineage. Very few people could claim kinship to the gods—they'd shown less and less interest in humans over the centuries, and now barely interfered in their lives at all.

"I would speak with you, Medusa, to learn the truth of your story, and to know of the wrongs done to you by my ancestor."

A golden light suddenly pierced the seal all along the edges of the box, beneath the lid. Cora's mouth fell open as Mrs. Harmon removed the top very slowly and set it aside. The conservatory was bathed in a magical glow. Cora squinted against the brightness until it slowly dimmed and she was able to look inside the box. She nearly fainted when she beheld its contents.

Inside was a severed head.

A severed head … with snakes for hair.

The skin was grey, cracked, and pulled tightly against the skull. Patches of thick scales trailed across the cheeks and forehead in wistful, swirling patterns. Within the deep sockets, the eyes were, mercifully, closed. At the removal of the lid, all of the snakes sprang upward with a chorus of hissing, fangs bared. Their sinuous bodies weaved in the air like sea grass, and they turned their heads to take in the faces hovering over them.

Cora had jumped back from the box upon seeing the head, but Mrs. Harmon's nose was only inches from the snake heads. As one, all of the serpents swiveled slowly to stare at her. The light from inside the box faded completely, but a glow remained in each of their eyes.

With a gulp, Cora moved to crouch cautiously next to her employer's chair, worried for her safety. She glanced up at the old woman's face and found no trace of fear there. Rather, she seemed mesmerized by the serpents swaying before her face. Cora turned her attention back to the head in the box, just as the lips parted and a soft voice began to speak in the Old Tongue.

"Daughter of Poseidon," Medusa whispered. "For too long have I lain in silence and darkness. I would tell you my story. But you must pledge me a favor of my choosing in return."

Medusa kept her eyes squeezed shut. The snakes settled back down into coils, brushing their scales against her sharp cheekbones.

Cora was about to ask what that favor would be, but before she could speak, Mrs. Harmon answered Medusa.

"I will grant you any favor you wish."

"Then listen, and when I have finished my story, I will ask it of you."

Cora's thighs were getting sore from crouching, so she tucked her legs underneath her, settling down onto the ground. She glanced nervously between the box and Mrs. Harmon's rapt face, wondering what the old lady had pledged herself to without a thought. What favor would a gorgon ask of a mortal?

It was too late to ask before Medusa began her tale.

"For years, I have listened. Muffled, through the sides of this box, I've heard the voices of generations of mortals.

I've been placed on mantles for decoration; I've been stored in warehouses and attics. And I've heard them tell my story to their children on more than one occasion. But they've always gotten it wrong ..."

I had many sisters. I was the youngest, and, according to many, the most beautiful. This worried my parents. They didn't have enough money to provide a decent dowry for me: therefore, my beauty was bound to only get me into trouble.

They considered it a great stroke of luck, then, when a priestess came from the temple of Athena to select new acolytes for the goddess of wisdom. The girls needed to be premium offerings: beautiful, intelligent, moral, and chaste. Any family that gave their daughter into the service of Athena would receive monetary compensation and increased social standing.

My parents did not hesitate to offer me up. I was selected the same day, and had to leave everything behind: all of my belongings, friends, and my dear sisters. We clung to each other and wept. The temple was far from our village; it was doubtful that I'd see them often, if at all. Priestesses could not leave the sacred grounds, and visits were rarely permitted.

As I walked behind the priestess's mule down the dusty road, I turned to look over my shoulder at our cottage for the last time. I had dreamt of living near my sisters, of holding their babies when theirs were born, and of having them hold mine. Our children would have played together. We would have sat on each other's porches to laugh and sing.

It took a week to reach the temple, and my feet were sore and blistered. The priestess hadn't spoken much to me throughout our journey, nor had she allowed me a turn on the mule at any point. She did not prepare me for my new life in any way, despite my many attempts at asking her questions.

I was never introduced to Athena herself, of course. She rarely visited, and when she did, I was kept busy in the kitchens, preparing her food. I was merely one of many virgin tributes to the goddess.

I had not been there long before he found me. I smelled him before I saw him. I was just coming out the front doors of the temple, holding my skirts to the side to make my way down the first step. It was broad daylight; the sun shone down on me with comforting warmth. I had only made it to the third step down when I caught a whiff of the ocean.

The odors of salt and fish met my nostrils, and I looked up curiously, as the shore was far away from the temple. He stood at the base of the stairs, watching me. I had not seen him approach.

Poseidon was the first god I ever saw, and there was no mistaking that he was immortal. He was enormous, and had a lustrous quality to his skin that was distinctly inhuman. His deep blue beard spilled down his chest in tight ringlets, adorned with pearls. I was brought to a halt by his otherworldly beauty, and stared at him, a doe trembling before a tiger.

He ascended toward me haughtily, raking his eyes over my body, making me blush. I backed up a step as he neared, but did not flee. It would have been an insult, and one did not insult a god.

Even standing on the step below me, he was still taller than I was. I looked up into his tanned face. He had the eyes of a shark, and when he smiled, I saw that his teeth were sharper than a human's.

"What a lovely little priestess," he rumbled, trailing a hand over my hair. "Why, your hair is even more beautiful than Athena's."

My eyes widened, but I said nothing. One did not argue with a god.

He chuckled, the sound rolling deep through his chest.

"You do not deny it," he said. "Such vanity!"

Before I could open my mouth to say something, his lips were upon mine. I had never been kissed before. I froze, unsure of what to do. I couldn't push him away. One did not refuse a god. So I let him kiss me, and I stayed still when his hands began to roam and he chuckled greedily.

He pushed me down on the steps and lifted my tunic. I closed my eyes as his tongue slithered down my throat.

One does not refuse a god, I reminded myself as he moved atop me, waves pounding against the shore, salt sweat dripping from his forehead.

A sound like the crack of thunder made my eyes fly open. Poseidon stood, leaving me splayed on the steps, the fabric of my tunic spread over the stone. He threw his head back and laughed at the darkening sky.

Athena stood at the very top of the steps, looking down at us with fire in her eyes. Her jaw clenched and she shook with rage as she raised a finger to point down at us. Poseidon merely kept laughing as he turned and walked back down the steps. That was when I realized that she was pointing a finger only at me.

"Foolish girl!" Athena cried.

She ran down the stairs to me, gripping me by the hair close to my scalp and yanking me to my feet. Tears stung my eyes as I looked up at her beautiful, terrible face for the first time. Her golden hair flowed through the air, though there was no breeze, and there seemed to be a golden glow about her. When she bared her teeth at me, I saw that they were every bit as sharp as Poseidon's.

"How dare you?! How *dare* you defile my temple with lust? How dare you forsake your sacred chastity?"

"But I—"

I didn't get to finish the sentence. She released my hair and slapped me. I fell down several steps, my cheek throbbing. I held it, crying, and looked up at her.

"You shall be punished for your crime, Medusa," she declared.

I shivered as she crept down the stairs toward me, her eyes dilated and focused on her prey. I thought to run, but knew that it would be useless. One did not run from a god. When her hand touched my hair again, I felt sharp prickles of pain all across my scalp. My eyes burned, and my skin felt as though it had been plunged into ice-cold water. I screamed and closed my eyes.

When I opened them again, I was alone, and I was no longer on the steps in the sunshine. It was pitch black, and the only sound was of a strange dripping echo, as though I were in a cave. I tried to rein in my panic, taking gasping, shuddering breaths, but just at that moment, something *slithered* over my shoulder.

A scream of terror ripped from my throat, and I stood and ran blindly. I tried to brush the thing off my shoulder, but merely felt it slide down my back. Then something touched my other shoulder, and I heard a low hissing sound. I tripped and fell heavily to the rough stone floor, skinning my hands and elbows.

I lay in the dark, and felt movement all over my head, over my shoulders, and down my back. The hissing grew louder. Cold scales brushed against the sore cheek that Athena had struck.

It took a long while for me to realize that the snakes were a part of me. It took me even longer to grapple in the dark until I finally found the mouth of the cave.

I emerged blinking into the light of the setting sun, my tunic torn and filthy, and looked down at my trembling hands. My skin was a strange greenish-grey, and the blood that beaded on my palms from my fall was black. I looked down at one of the snakes. It looked back up at me, tongue flickering out, and my heart skipped a beat. In the light, I could see that each snake was a different species. There were adders and cobras, and brightly-striped coral snakes, as well. Each seemed to move of its own free will, its own creature, but none of them hurt me.

I looked around me. My cave was halfway up a barren mountain on a small island. The sea stretched out to the horizon, and every wave that hit the cliffs below made me flinch. There was a flash of green light as the sun set, and then darkness consumed me.

It was nearly a year before I saw another person. I had learned to hunt the small animals that lived on the island, and found that I could eat them raw with my new, sharp fangs. My snakes were my only companions, and I spoke to them and sang to them as I moved restlessly about the land.

Never did I step foot on the one small portion of beach, let alone in the water. The sea was Poseidon, and Poseidon was the sea. I did not ever want to feel his touch again. I hated the ocean, and every single creature in it.

Therefore, I did not immediately know it when a boat came to my island. I was asleep, deep in the cave, surrounded by the bones of my last meal. My tunic had long since worn away, and I was comfortable with my skin. As time passed, it became more covered with scaly patches.

I had become monstrous, and it was a monster that the sailors saw the next morning when I found them camping near the beach. I wandered amongst their tents, baffled by the sudden presence of other people, and was just reaching to wake one of them when I heard a scream behind me.

I whirled around to see a man staring at me, mouth agape and eyes wide with horror. The instant my gaze fell upon him … he turned to stone. More shouts came from behind me, and I turned to look at those men, too.

Their skin crackled and froze, paling to grey. Even their eyelashes turned to tiny slivers of stone. They gaped like fish as they struggled against the spreading. One of them left their mouth agape, as though to scream, and I watched the stone spread up his throat, cutting off his breath with sharp, painful stabs.

There was no doubt in my mind that they were not dying peacefully. Expressions of agony graced each of their faces.

I met all of their gazes until I was surrounded by a crew of statues. Everything was silent once again, though it seemed as though the air still rung with the screams of the newly dead. I heard only the seabirds crying above, and the infernal, incessant pulsing of the waves. Covering my ears, tears flowing freely down my face, I ran from the terrible sound.

The years passed. Sometimes visitors would come to my island, but they were few and far between. Once or twice, a few lived to escape, and thus my story spread. Soon, men fancying themselves to be heroes began to seek me out, hoping to bring back my head as a trophy.

Those men I dragged to stand vigil at the mouth of my cave after I looked upon them. They stood, rigid sentinels against the sea and a warning to any other foolish enough to come looking for me. I began to relish turning men to stone.

It was in this state that Perseus finally found me. He was a handsome young man with curling auburn hair—the type I would have found attractive before my life was ruined by the gods and their games. I knew he was different from the ones who'd come before. He bore with him gifts from the gods: a sword and a magical pouch. On his feet were sandals from Hermes. Worst of all, though, he carried the shield of Athena.

My head spun and my heart clenched. How could the gods have given him everything, while leaving me to rot in a cave? What had I done to deserve my fate? What had *he* done to deserve *his*? My mind whirled and my chest felt as though it were weighted down by stone.

When I saw that token from my former mistress, I was taken aback and just distracted enough by my heartbreak and jealousy for Perseus to land that fatal blow that severed my head from my body. After the crack of pain, I thought only of relief and release as I fell to the floor, my vision rolling until I was looking back at my own naked, terrifying body.

A pool of black blood was seeping from my severed neck. Perseus was moving toward me, a sack in his hands. I expected my vision to fade at any moment. Surely, I'd only be aware for a few seconds at most after being beheaded?

But no.

I continued to see and hear as Perseus stopped next to me. My snakes hissed in outrage as he reached down to lift me into that dark sack. I hoped they would bite him, but he moved too quickly. I was stuffed down to feel the rough fabric rub irritatingly against my nose, and the sack was tied off. He slung me over his shoulder, and I bumped painfully against his back as he strode out of my cave. If I could have cried, I would have, knowing I'd never walk again, never feel grass between my toes or flower petals beneath

118

my fingertips. Was this to be my fate? A severed head with a sliver of awareness? A trophy for Perseus? Oh, what a curse Athena had laid upon me! And all because Poseidon used me to insult her vanity.

When Perseus reached the mouth of the cave, he ran down until he came to the edge of a cliff, then leapt into the air. The sensation was strange, to say the least. I was dizzy, but could feel no nausea, no drop in my non-existent stomach.

We flew for a long time. I listened to the smooth flapping of the wings on the sandals, and contemplated my fate. Where was this young man taking me? Was I to be a trophy for some king, or was I being brought to Athena? Or worse … Poseidon.

If I could have shivered, I would have. I felt some of the last drops of my black blood leak out the corners of my mouth and tried desperately to catch them with the tip of my tongue. The coppery tang was sharp, but then faded, and soon, I was bloodless. My skin instantly felt drier, as though it were pinched and more prone to cracking.

Gradually, I became aware of the sound of distant roars and splashing. The sounds grew louder. Perseus was descending toward the source. As we got closer, I could feel the hot breath of an enormous creature. It sounded as though it were crawling awkwardly over a sandbar. The stench of rotting fish hit my nostrils, and I deeply wished I could pinch them together to block it out.

With a jolt, Perseus landed on what I assumed was the shore. It sounded like his sandals hit a rocky surface. All was dark in the sack as I listened and tried to piece together what was happening around me. I heard the drawstrings being tugged open.

Ah, I thought. *He intends to use me to kill this fell beast.*

I heard the giant creature splash more as it crested the sandbar and continued toward where Perseus was standing. A hand reached in and grabbed me by my serpentine tresses, yanking me out into the light. His touch reminded me of that last morning in my home, when my father swept my hair back from my face and told me I would be a beautiful tribute to Athena. He'd known very well that I wished to marry and stay with my family, but he merely smiled blandly in the face of my sobs. No matter what I'd said, he'd kept that smile pasted on his lips.

I squeezed my eyes shut. I was determined in that moment to keep them closed and let the monster devour us both. Spray from the sea hit my cheeks, making me snarl with anger, baring my fangs.

But then, I heard her screams.

Heavy chains clinked against rock, and the grunts of a struggling woman reached my ears. A virgin sacrifice. Undoubtedly, her foolish village was offering her up to appease the monster headed straight for us. This poor girl's parents had given her up to an even worse fate than mine had.

Perseus did not notice that my eyes were closed as he hoisted me high above his head, facing the sea and the incoming threat. The salt of the ocean mist stung the flesh of my severed, exposed neck. I heard the creature roar hungrily as it approached, and the girl's terrified shrieks.

I could not let her be devoured by this child of Poseidon's.

I opened my eyes.

The creature was hideous, perhaps even more so than myself. It had vestigial limbs that it was using to haul itself through the shadows. Its flesh was smooth and blubbery over a massive frame, and the oversized head was equipped with strong jaws and ten-inch-long teeth. A whip-like tail lashed in the water behind it to a frothy foam. Its eyes were beady and sunken- the creature clearly relied mostly on its sense of smell, for its long snout was topped by nostrils large enough for a man to curl in.

It had been close enough to strike when I opened my eyes and met its unintelligent gaze. The stone spread from the eyes and down the rest of its body with a series of crackling noises as organs were transformed. The body sank into the sand with its new weight, though most of it still jutted above the surface of the water, poised as though to attack.

I heard the girl gasp and then begin sobbing with relief behind me, and allowed my eyes to close once more. Exhaustion overtook me as Perseus hurriedly stuffed me back into the sack, eager to get to the woman. As soon as I was securely tied, he dropped me to the hard ground and I saw stars behind my eyelids. My snakes hissed at the impact and writhed in pain and fury. Everything went black.

When I awoke again, we were flying once more. I could hear Perseus talking to the girl and calling her Princess Andromeda. She had been a very expensive virgin sacrifice indeed, then. Her voice was soft and still trembled slightly from shock as she answered his questions. It was clear that he was quite enamored of her.

Again we touched down, this time on a dirt path, and I bumped along in the bag as Perseus walked briskly and with determination. Princess Andromeda walked with us. I could hear her lighter footfalls on the road, following Perseus.

By and by, Perseus came to an abrupt halt.

"Release me, old man!" he huffed. "I am on an important errand!"

"Beware!" came the voice of an elder. "Beware, young Perseus, for the King wishes you dead!"

With a hiss, I opened my eyes. I could not be fooled by the glamour. This was the voice of Athena. She had disguised herself as an old man in order to warn this fool Perseus.

He must indeed be a darling of the gods, I thought, *to merit such extravagant interference in his affairs.*

Perseus shrugged off the old man and continued up the path. His sandals soon slapped against smooth marble, and the sound echoed off walls and columns. We were in a palace, then.

Gradually, the murmur of arguing men grew to a roar as Perseus entered a chamber or meeting hall. As he came into their view, all fell silent.

"Stay here," I heard him whisper to Andromeda, "and do not watch."

Then he strolled across the room, bringing the sack I was in to the front of his body, no doubt drawing everyone's attention to it. I growled. There were gasps of outrage as Perseus drew closer to his goal.

"What are you doing here?!" a deep voice roared.

Perseus halted, clearly taken aback.

Idiot, I thought. *You really thought they would welcome you? Any man who had been sent after me had clearly been issued a death sentence. They weren't banking on your return, Perseus.*

"King Polydectes, I have brought you the head of Medusa!" Perseus declared.

"LIAR!!!" the deep voice shouted.

That voice ... it reminded me of Poseidon's. I gritted my teeth.

Perseus began to untie the sack. I opened my eyes and grinned like the feral creature I was. I wanted to kill a king.

"If there is anyone here who thinks of me as a friend, please look away now!" Perseus thundered as he brought me into the open.

I barely had a chance to see what the king looked like before he turned grey under my gaze, along with all of the men standing around him. Their clothes hung on their newly-statuesque forms, sandals pinned beneath a much heavier weights.

Perseus shoved me unceremoniously into the sack, and then walked to set me on the empty throne across the room. I listened from my illustrious seat as men argued.

Eventually, Perseus was declared king, and he asked Andromeda to be his queen.

The rest of that day is a blur in my memory. I spent most of my time contemplating an existence with no body. I was consumed with hatred and fear, thinking of how Athena had cursed me to not only a lifetime of solitude, but an eternity. Could anything destroy me?

Eventually, the bag was lifted and I was transferred to a crate. This was then moved to a store room and put under guard. I tried everything to make the time pass more quickly. I even attempted to speak to the guards that I could hear nearby, but that only made them stand farther away.

I do not know whether it was day or night when Andromeda first came to speak with me. She dismissed the guards and stood next to the table where my crate sat. I heard her lay her hands on the box.

"Medusa, I thank you for saving me from sacrifice. I know you cannot hear me, but I am sorry that your death preserved my life."

The lid of the crate creaked open, and she grasped the bag to lift me out. Untying the drawstring, she reached a trembling hand in to pull me up by my snakes, which turned docile under her touch. I squeezed my eyes shut, afraid to turn her to stone, though I suspect her eyes were closed, as well.

She put me into a new box almost reverently, and sealed the lid with a spell she had purchased from a cave prophetess. Only a descendant of hers with truth in their heart would be able to open the box.

Cora blinked, then turned to look at Mrs. Harmon in awe.

"But then ..."

"Yes," Medusa said, "Doris is a Daughter of Poseidon, and also of Andromeda. She carries blood from both of their lines in her veins."

Mrs. Harmon looked just as surprised as Cora felt.

"I never knew ..." she whispered.

Both women stared at the head in silence before Cora ventured a question.

"What ... what is the favor you wish to have granted?"

"I want revenge."

It took Cora months to find a descendant of Hermes who would be able to contact the god. With sheer luck, a mutual friend introduced her to his son, and the two instantly connected. She began seeing him frequently, and they made each other happy. So, when she asked him for the favor of a conversation with his father, he was only too happy to facilitate the meeting.

When Hermes arrived, the room was bathed in the golden glow from his skin. He fixed Cora with a penetrating gaze, then smiled.

His teeth were like thorns.

"What can I do for you, young lady?" he asked, eyebrows raised and hands placed on his son's shoulders.

His son answered the question.

"Father, this is Cora, my girlfriend," he said. "She has a favor to ask of you."

Hermes smiled, but said nothing, waiting for Cora to elaborate. She had fetched a parcel, wrapped in brown paper, from her car before the visit. Now, she brought it onto her lap.

"My employer, Mrs. Harmon, is a Daughter of Poseidon. She is dying, and wishes to give a gift of tribute to her great Father before her passing. Could you please deliver it to him?"

Hermes took the offering with no hesitation. After an enjoyable evening and dinner together, the god departed, flying off the doorstep, carrying the box. Cora watched him go, willing him to reach his goal, so that Poseidon might finally see what awaited him.

Poseidon had come ashore to pursue pleasures of the flesh. He had tired of rutting with the creatures of the deep, and wished to hold a human woman in his arms again. It had been many years since he had come up from the waves.

The bordello was a high-end establishment, and he commanded that it shut down to every other customer for the night. He wanted them all to himself. Time passed quickly, and afterwards, he lay exhausted on a bed, shooing the last of the women away. Fifty times in one night was a new personal record. He sighed and closed his eyes, but then started at a knock on his window. Poseidon stood, naked, and opened the window. Hermes hovered outside, carrying a strange parcel.

"This is a tribute from one of your descendants, Poseidon," the messenger god said.

With a grunt, Poseidon took the box and shooed Hermes away rudely. Then he turned to set the box on a table, and collapsed back on the bed to sleep.

The next morning, it was the first thing he saw when he opened his eyes. Feeling rested, his curiosity piqued, Poseidon began to unwrap it.

Inside was a beautiful golden box. It was carved all over with images of the sea and its creatures. His home. He made a small noise of appreciation.

Poseidon opened the box.

Medusa opened her eyes.

Book III

A Bedtime Story

by Deborah Markus

Silly warriors. You always think you'll catch me sleeping.

Fair's fair. I *was* asleep.

But *they* weren't.

A word from the wise: struggling like that just makes them hold on tighter.

Strong, aren't they? And longer than you expected them to be, I'll bet.

I was surprised by that myself, at first.

Hey.

Hey!

Oh, for—look. No, *look*. At ME.

Fine. Don't.

I'm just saying, you were lied to. I don't turn men to stone. And I'm not ugly.

Other than the hair thing, which I admit takes some getting used to.

I find it wonderful myself, but then I'm the one who used to have to do all that brushing and combing.

Once upon a time, I had the longest, most beautiful tresses the world had ever seen.

Now I have freedom.

And friends!

But sure—squinch your eyes shut if it makes you feel better.

Can I just ask one question?

Who exactly would be able to report the "fact" that looking at me turns men to stone? I mean, maybe metaphorically. Anyone catching sight of me unawares is going to be stunned for a second.

Frozen by surprise and fear. Understandably. But turned into an actual *rock*? That's just crazy talk.

You don't look convinced.

You'd rather believe some stranger's tale than take my word about my own life?

Typical. Men write stories. Women have to live them.

And when the lives don't match the stories, *we're* the ones who must be doing it wrong.

Are you going to lie there with your eyes screwed shut for the rest of your life?

Suit yourself.

Could you at least tell me your name?

Fine. I'll call you Per. Short for Per Usual.

And since you're not feeling chatty, I'll tell you my story. The *real* story.

But first I'll tell you yours.

Let me guess. Athena loaned you a shield and told you to polish it until it shone like glass. That way, you could use it as a mirror so you wouldn't have to look at me while you chopped my head off.

The things some gods will do to get out of cleaning their own armor.

Anyway. She said she'd help you become a hero, right? By murdering a woman in her sleep. A woman whose hair was once her crowning beauty.

Not that *I* was the one who used to brag about it. That was my dad.

He wanted to marry me off, of course. That's what fathers do when they're unlucky enough to have daughters instead of sons.

And since I was—if you'll pardon the phrase—drop-dead gorgeous, he thought he'd be able to get away with a skimpy dowry. I played along with my father's plans to buy myself some time. I smiled and fawned and suggested we put off choosing my husband until my hair reached my feet. Between that and my family name, he'd have suitors *clamoring* for my hand. And if any of them made a

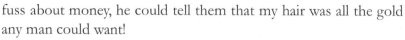

fuss about money, he could tell them that my hair was all the gold any man could want!

It worked.

I was seventeen before he started getting insistent. All my friends had been married for years by then.

I had the chance to see what *that* was like. And I didn't want it. I didn't want to be shut away from the world like treasure in a chest. I didn't want to rot in some man's mansion while he got to have adventures and I got to have babies until I died. That's what happened to my mother. And her mother.

So I told my father the truth. I didn't want to get married. I wanted to be a priestess. Dad wasn't having it. I was his only shot at grandchildren. Gotta keep that male line going, even if it skips a stitch here or there! I hauled out my best wheedling and coaxing, but it didn't work. I was getting married and that was that. When I tried to argue, he said that if religion was so important to me, I could celebrate the Thesmophoria once a year like all the other girls.

I wanted to say that it wasn't about religion. It was about freedom. Instead, I bowed my head. Mostly to hide my expression.

I was hatching a plan.

I would go to Athena's temple that night. If anyone saw me, I'd say I was bringing an offering. Which was true. But it wasn't wheat, or wine, or weaving. You can guess what I was *really* offering, right?

Per? Can you guess? Or maybe you want to save your breath for, well, breathing. Sounds like it's getting a little tight there.

Anyway. I was going to give the goddess my long golden hair. I figured Athena would love that. For a goddess of war and wisdom, she can be surprisingly shallow sometimes. You heard about that beauty contest she entered, right? I knew she'd appreciate me making myself less gorgeous. And she was all for women not getting married, especially if they wanted to spend their time singing songs about *her*.

I'd dropped some hints to the priestesses already. I knew they'd be happy to take me in. And without all that splendiferous hair, I'd be a lot harder to marry off.

I really thought it would work. And It might have, if Athena had been the only god involved that night.

Unfortunately, Poseidon saw me sneak out.

I'd seen him once or twice, from a distance. He's the god of oceans. I lived on an island. He was hard to miss. He'd noticed me, too. Even when I was just a girl. I was a grown woman now. And I'd left the safety of my father's house. I was fair game. If I didn't like it, I should have stayed home.

I heard him following me. I glanced back and wished I hadn't. I knew from the look on his face what would happen next. It would be awful, and it would be the end of any chance I had for *any* kind of life.

The priestesses might sympathize, but they wouldn't be able to welcome me into the order. This was a virgins-only club.

I wouldn't be marriageable, either. Suitors wanted a fresh, unopened package, and Poseidon was bound to brag that I was anything but. Plus, sex with a god would leave me pregnant. Probably with something weird. If my father didn't kill me, giving birth to a litter of sea-horses might.

I hitched up my skirts and ran straight to the temple. He couldn't do anything to me *there*. Could he?

It might have worked if this had been the temple of another god. As it was, this was Mr. Splashy's big chance to get back at that uppity little virgin-goddess who'd beaten him out of naming rights to the greatest city in Greece. And made him look like a big useless blowhard in the process.

I'm not boring you, am I? Your eyes are really glazing over.

Well. I managed to get inside the temple. Poseidon followed me in. And told me exactly what he planned to do next. If a senior god wanted to break the rules, there wasn't much anyone could do about it. Athena could complain to her dad after, but that wouldn't help *me* any.

Fortunately, I was begging protection from the goddess of wisdom. And I was being pursued by someone who wasn't interested in my sparkling personality. Athena couldn't stop him from taking me, but she could do her best to make him not want to.

Okay, she might have overdone it. But honestly? These snakes are pretty cool. Athena even gave me the power to speak their language. So quite aside from my new look, I always have company, and I have a beautiful island to call my own. Athena set that up, too. No bossy fathers, no pesky suitors, no prison-marriage or pregnancies. Just fresh air and freedom, and the occasional idiot.

That's you, by the way.

Will you PLEASE just open your eyes?

Fine. I'll do it for you.

There. See? I'm not so awful to look at. And you're still flesh and blood. All that talk of turning men to stone is a pack of lies. For all I know, my father came up with that story to get back at me for not being a good little girl.

What are you looking at?

Those? Those aren't dead heroes. They're rocks.

Now, those weird husk-looking things over there? *Those* are dead men. If I'd known company was coming, I'd have cleaned up. Seriously. Did you think you were the first one Athena ever lured over here?

Right. You thought this trip was *your* idea.

Oh, honey.

The priestesses brought me here after the incident. Athena showed them the way. Athena is the only one who can show the way here. It's a wonderful, welcoming place.

I could probably get by just fine on fruit and fish. But the priestesses bring me things. Bread. Wine. Incense to honor my goddess.

Everything I need.

Everything *I* need.

But—well, my reptile accessories don't need to eat too often. But they do need to eat *big*. Which is where you come in, Per.

There you go writhing again. So dramatic. Like I said, I can't turn you to stone. But a bite from my new hairdo will make you feel as if I had.

Just for a little while.

Just until you stop feeling anything at all.

My goodness. I'm exhausted from so much talking. And I can't go back to bed until my beautiful friends finish their dinner. So if it's all the same to you, I'll just sit down and let them get to it.

Goodnight.

The Coming of Perseid

by April Yates

They say I turn men into stone.

What they mean is that I turn a small part of them to stone.

They cast me from Athena's temple when Poseidon's lust for me turned into a grotesque display of his power.

They like to blame me—women as well sometimes—when men lose control of themselves.

They say I turn men into stone.

That must be why they have sent this girl in her ill-fitting armour. Who drops her sword, shivering and moaning, when I caress her.

Yes, I turn men into stone, but it seems I turn women into water.

The Original Nasty Woman

by Theresa Derwin

I saunter towards the kiosk, the smell of freshly made popcorn—cloyingly sweet—luring me in. The lights are bright and glaring, a good excuse to wear my tinted glasses. As a group of giggling girls finish their order and trot towards the screens, I find, in front of me, a wonderful specimen of youth; barely out of his teens, he is pimply, and gangly, unsure of his own body and when he sees me, I grimace. Here we go again.

"Whu whu. What can I getcha Miss?"

If it's possible, his face becomes even redder; an explosion of tomatoes.

"Just a large Diet Coke please."

You don't retain my figure for thousands of years without a few sacrifices.

He stumbles to fill my order and finally I have my drink and off I go to watch an absolute classic that always makes me seethe with anger and bad memories.

Clash of the Titans.

I'm just at the part where Medusa slithers out, the snakes on her head writhing and hissing, and I wish I'd bought snacks so I could throw them at the screen.

Harryhausen was talented, but he'd obviously had issues with the women in his life.

This thought is interrupted by a cluster of popcorn flying past my head towards the screen. "What the—"

I snap my head round, about to tear into the enthusiastic critic, when the scent of ripe sweat, angst, fear and hormones hits me.

The rank scent comes from the row behind me, occupied by lanky, lazy layabout boys, sprawled across the seats like rejects from *West Side Story*.

And pinned between them is the source of the heightened fear.

Like hyenas, they'd found a potential victim sitting on her own and surrounded her; caging her in.

Isn't that what most boys do to young women?

My tongue flicks out, briefly tasting the myriad of aromas.

Like recognises like. Beneath the girl's fear, I can smell lemon groves, salty skin, warm breezes and hot nights.

She's a radiant little thing in her late teens; warm olive skin, deep brown eyes and a mass of dark curls pulled over her face like a shield. The shield I wear is an elaborate peacock silk scarf to hide my curls.

"Hmmph. Boys. If I were you, I would leave quietly and quickly before I show you what it's like when a girl fights back."

The pasty one with dirty blond hair snorts. "Ya can try luv, but there's four of us and ... HOLY FUCK!"

I stand and yank him close to me, smiling as my forked tongue slips out and tastes the boy's noxious skin.

"Mmm, you taste like chicken," I lie.

His milk-toned skin drains of colour, turning an even paler shade of polished bone.

Surprisingly the girl just sits, gawping, as my eyes flicker between green and yellow.

Then the boys run. The urge to follow, to hunt, almost overwhelms me.

The added smell of fresh urine tangles with my senses. Prey.

No. Stay. Protect.

I stay.

Yak. Horrible creatures.

Perseus and Medusa continue to battle on screen, oblivious to my presence.

"What's your name girl?" I ask.

"Arianna," she whispers, with a soft Mediterranean accent.

"Beautiful name. I knew an Arianna once," I tell her, "though you do not look like you have eight legs."

I laugh and she shudders slightly.

I'm still surprised she hasn't run. She is a brave one.

"Come, I will not harm you. We are all daughters of the goddesses and we must help each other with our trials."

She nods, then smiles awkwardly.

Grabbing a glittery unicorn backpack, she stands up and I see a hint of the daughter I was never allowed to have.

"Eese omorefe." You are beautiful, I tell her. I dreamed of having such a daughter.

"Sas efcharisto." Thank you.

Through the bustle of the foyer, we make our escape into the fresh night air. Arianna is shaking and I quickly guide her towards a small pub hidden on a darkened side street.

It isn't long before I sip a chilled, white wine and I convince Arianna to join me.

Liam will not ask questions of his clientele in here. We are all unique; all hidden or hunted by our past.

He has owned the tavern for a couple of centuries now. He is one of the old Celtic gods, long forgotten though he does not seem to care.

He enjoys what he calls the 'banter', the beer, the whiskey and the women.

I should be offended but I know that is just the mask he wears; the easygoing Irish lad who will do no harm. Until you mess with him, that is. It's a lovely place; all varnished wood, cosy fire-lit corners, faux gas lanterns and the chink of glasses amidst a background of laughter and song.

"You know your mother tongue then?" I ask.

She laughs. "Yaya tried to reach me as a kid. I used to think 'thank you' was 'a fairy's toe'. For years I was convinced I was thanking the fairies."

I laugh with her.

The wine has restored her colour a bit and she is much brighter without the constant fear hanging over her. I wonder why the insolent boys were following her.

"You mentioned your Yaya. What about your mother?"

"I never knew her. She left when I was little. Went off to find a singing career. Ended up drunk and working at holiday camps, last I heard."

"I'm sorry," I say, "I had sisters once, until they were taken from me. I know what it is to lose family. Especially the women in our family."

"It is what it is," she says, though I see the hint of pain in her eyes.

We all wear masks. Especially us women.

We have sat for about an hour, chatting about everything and anything when I ask about the boys who were following her.

"Ugh, that's Eli and his crew. Thinks he's a hard ass and he likes to stalk me for cheap thrills and scares," she tells me.

"I could take care of it," I tell her. "A simple solution. Not like the old days though."

"Oh?"

"Oh yes, child. I remember the good old days when we used to sacrifice our king to fructify the land; with a dash of poison on a spear, or a by roasting him on a lovely pyre before dinner. Didn't matter how he died, but die he must. Perhaps that is what is wrong with our society now? What do you think, girl?"

She splutters her drink and I laugh, my babies hissing along with me from under my scarf.

"Okay," she says, "hit me with it. Are you her? Am I blind drunk or imagining it all or … and how are you alive? I mean …"

She took a gulp of her drink and I nod at Liam.

Refills turn up quickly and I pat his calloused hand in thanks.

"So, Arianna, you want the truth?"

Another swig of the fizzy stuff, then "Yeah, I do. Please, Me—miss? Ma'am?"

I take a healthy swig of my own drink, a sharp memory of pain stabbing me in the chest.

In my heart.

This will hurt, but they say that the truth hurts.

"A transaction then. Call me Firosa. It is a fitting name for me now. Tell me—"

"What, Furiosa like *Mad Max*? She rocks."

I hear Liam chuckle and shake my head.

"I have no idea of this Furiosa, girl. I am Firosa. Now, about the noisome boys. The ones who follow you."

I think the whole bar can hear her pained sigh.

She's weary of it all; tired of being attacked, stalked, of unwanted hands on her flesh. I recognise the look.

Eli had started sniffing around her a few weeks ago at school, teasing her, following and poking fun at her.

It started with name calling.

Then kicking her backpack.

It turned out it was the late teen boy equivalent of pulling hair.

Ari remembered the day Eli had asked her out in the canteen, and his shock when she'd laughed in his face, which burned red and hot.

In front of his friends.

It wasn't long after that he and his snivelling hyenas were telling her to "go back to your own country."

She'd been born in England for fuck sake.

Her mistake had been yelling back at them.

Arianna's body was rigid against the alley wall; taut with fear.

Eli, Mark and Jake surrounded her, Eli's heavy frame pushing his erection into her.

"Shut up, bitch."

Instead, she screamed, loudly, and Raju from the corner shop had heard, scaring the boys off with his broom. The next day she'd skipped school and hidden in the cinema, where Firosa had found her.

I hiss, and my babies join in with their chorus of anger.

"Malako. I am so sorry girl, but trust me on this. What happened today, it will not happen again. This, I swear to you."

"Sas efcharisto."

"Is good. Now, you have earned my story. Settle in. What do you know of the legends?"

"Yaya told me some stories but most of them I learnt from, well, *Clash of the Titans*."

I cringe and it makes Arianna laugh.

"Sorry. But you know, just the main things. Perseus slay you and took your head, you turn people into stone. Both obvs not real. And you had an affair with Poseidon and were supposed to have kids but ... um."

"It is okay," I tell her. "History is told by the victors. And of course, they do not call it his-story for nothing."

She laughs at my little joke and her face becomes sunshine again.

"I had no affair with Poseidon. I had no choice with him. But always, it is the woman who is blamed, no? Even by her sisters. And it is woman who is punished. As for my eyes? Well, I think a demonstration is in order. Liam?"

Suddenly Liam is beside me, and I scent the beast beneath his skin, waiting to burst out.

All of us here, in this little pub, we are the forgotten, the hidden, and we protect each other.

"Bring my gift for our sweet Arianna, please."

Liam slips away, quiet and deadly.

Francis bolts the front door and a few of the clientele shift to pull down the blinds. Alan puts the jukebox on loud, with some rock song to cover the sounds anyone might hear.

Arianna and I have been here long enough for me to discreetly text him about the boys, about their supposed leader, Eli.

I can smell his fear, and the acrid stench of piss and vomit before Eli is dragged into the pub lounge by a snarling Liam.

He is gagged and wearing a blindfold.

Arianna gasps and I hold her hand, keeping her still, though her pulse jumps beneath my touch.

"Shhh, it is okay, girl. Is good."

Liam removes the blindfold, the gag, throws the boy to the floor in front of me, and the boy whimpers.

When he sees Arianna, his eyes widen then he starts begging her.

"Ari, tell 'em to let me go. I'm sorry. I'm sorry. I'm sorry I'm sorry I'm sorry."

All words stop as I unwrap my scarf, release my writhing babies —and stare into his eyes.

"You're not gonna kill—kill him?" Arianna asks.

I smile, showing fang, then laugh.

"No, child. Did I not explain? My powers do not turn people into stone. But if I wish, my babies can cause temporary paralysis."

I open my newfangled phone that Liam and Alan made me buy.

It's the next morning and Liam has sent me one of those photo messages. What's happening, I think it is called.

I open it and burst out laughing.

Liam, he is a good friend and a good man.

I am laughing so hard I can hardly breathe, and my babies are bouncing up and down on my head with merriment.

Arianna's school courtyard has a new statue present.

It is white, pasty, wears a laurel wreath on its head, is posed like Cupid and is wearing an adult diaper.

His eyes are open wide in shock and no doubt he is very chilly after a night spent naked on school grounds. He is surrounded by his crew and a myriad of teens taking photos on their phone. The last photo Liam sends me is of Arianna, her smile so wide it brightens the day.

This is so much fun.

Much better than eating the boy, though my babies might disagree with that.

Stony Overdrafts

by Jason P. Burnham

MonoMastys: one new notification.

Medusa opened the phone app.

You have one new super-premium subscriber. Want to welcome them?

She checked her account settings again, making sure super-premiums were auto-billed monthly. They would be.

Verified PindarofThebes490's debit card.

A thrill of anticipation ran through her.

Low- and medium-tier videos never showed her face—they were teasers to entice super-premium subscriptions.

She found the video of her staring into the camera for a full minute and sent it to *PindarofThebes490*.

She wondered how many monthly payments she could bleed from a stone before the card got canceled.

She blushed. And hissed.

Classic Medusa. © 2022 Chaz Kemp. All rights reserved.

Snakes and Stones

by Claire McNerney

My mother, the stone woman, has been in love since the day my father kissed her porcelain body into being. I swore I would never be like her: person-less, soulless, only in love, nothing without it. My father is a lover too—worse, he is an artist. He carved my mother and perhaps he carved me, though I do not love him like she does, so I doubt I am his design.

There is a snake woman (only a girl, really) who lives in the caves. She lets me bring her apples and cakes of honey. I cannot gaze upon her—she will not let me—but from the sound of her voice alone I know she is beautiful. I know she is cursed, too, like Daphne, like Echo. It is a curse of loneliness, I think. If it were up to me, she would never be lonely.

She never leaves her cave. I hear the snakes whisper awful things to her when they think I cannot hear them. She never responds, but some days I think that I can hear her nodding along. 'Yes, I am hideous. Yes, I am unlovable. Yes, I brought this upon myself.' As if it was her fault her uncle took her to the temple that day and let the gods open her up and leave her hollow.

Today, her voice is not there to greet mine. I toss a honey cake wrapped in cloth into the cave, but her arm does not reach out of the shadows to collect it.

"Medusa?" I shout, "Are you alright?" But I hear nothing.

I walk in—how could I not? When we first met, she told me to never enter this cave when she was in it. But without any sound, not even that of snoring or breathing, I cannot be sure that she is still there.

On my way, I pick up the cake as an excuse to go further.

Deep in the cave, I cannot see more than a few feet ahead of me. The stone wall is the same temperature as my skin. Is it warm, or am I cold? I shout her name again, then I see it on the ground: a dead snake. One of hers.

I continue, forwards, following the trail of tail-less, bloody snakes, beheaded from her head. I fear what I may find in the dark at the end of the path. Herhead, gone? That is how the story goes. Her body, empty once again? She does not deserve to bear such pain.

Out of the silence, I hear sobbing. I whisper her name as I round the corner. Then I see her. Her head is bald and bloody, a pile of snakes around her. Her face is messy and wet, her red hands curled around her body.

When she looks up at me, I am stuck in place.

"You." Her eyes are wide and beautiful, but they are full of fear. "Not you, too. Not you."

I am shocked to feel my heartbeat, to hear my breath. She is too distracted by her pain to see me blink once, twice. I move towards her, cautiously. Mouth gaping with awe, she reaches out, and I get to touch her hand for the first time. She wraps it around mine, and despite the drying blood it is so soft. My stiff fingers warm in hers.

If I am now stone, I was born stone. That may be my burden, but it will never be hers. I will hold it just as I hold her now, surrounded by the snakes that no longer trap her. I wrap my arms around Medusa and listen to her heart beating.

The Gravel Menagerie

by Marisca Pichette

Our daughter's first pet
was a rock the size of a snail.

Her second pet took
the shape of a mole.

It rested beside her bed,
her midnight snores hissing a lullaby.

Stone mosquitos dusted the sheets
disrupted by her breaths.

Beside the mole, a stone garter snake
when she was seven—her favorite.

She wore it twined
in her living hair.

Her bedroom filled with stone ferrets,
songbirds, mink & beaver.

When she left for college
her pets gathered venom & dust.

Mosquitos buzzed in the night.

She returned a woman
pulling a wagon in her wake.
Her latest pet: a man.

She found a corner & stood him
facing her bed, rock eyes wide
mouth closed.

The mosquitos stilled to pebbles in her eyes
& she slept

in silence.

The Ayes Have It

by Gordon Linzner

Margaret Duchet peered over the top of her emerald-tinted glasses as she settled into her usual seat in the first row of the spectators' gallery in the main courtroom at the Old Bailey. The chamber's gas lamps seemed dimmer than usual this morning, likely a result of the effect of the day's thicker than usual pea-soup fog on her sensitive eyes as she'd strode through the busy London streets.

Duchet stroked her chin in contemplation as the courtroom slowly filled. Many faces looked familiar, which meant she too stood out, even with her disguises. She and her confidant Penelope would soon have to leave London for different part of the world.

Again.

Her sensitive fingers drifted over faint jawline scars. Doctor Asclepius had intended to remove those as he had the more dramatic disfigurations while restoring her face; she chose to retain them to reminder her how easily, often unjustifiably, her fellow gods were offended. She had also learned, over the past two millennia, that such minor defects could underscore, rather than undermine, one's natural beauty.

Duchet toyed briefly with her glasses before sitting back, arms folded across her bodice. Enduring the Victorian-era legal process was the most tedious part of her obligation to humanity, but worth the results. This was day two of the trial of Richard Carter, accused of murdering of his common-law wife, Charlotte Ellis. The evidence against him was slim and, unlike too many other defendants, Carter could afford a decent barrister. As of yesterday afternoon, both judge and jury seemed leaning towards acquittal.

Duchet, with her centuries of experience in reading people of every class, was far less certain of that decision.

Carter was called to the stand.

Duchet paid little heed to his testimony, concentrating on the man's actions rather than his words, even as she made faint gestures to gain his attention. When she finally succeeded in catching his eye, through use of both her beauty and demeanor, it was for but a moment.

That moment was all she needed.

She lowered the tinted glasses, fixing the defendant with her dazzling blue eyes.

Cold blue eyes, brighter than any gas lamp in the chamber.

Penetrating.

Soul-rending.

Carter froze in the middle a sentence. He rose to his feet in the witness box, to stand stiff as a statue. His fingers whitened as they gripped the wooden railing.

He turned to the jurors, lips twisting, face flushed red with anger.

"I'll not pretend any longer!" he shouted. Even the judge leaned back at the outburst.

"She asked for it!" Carter went on. "Bashed her head in with a pipe, I did! Stuffed the thing under the floorboards in the bedroom, wrapped in my bloodstained robe, where no one would think to look! I'd do it again, too!"

The defendant's body suddenly went slack, like a punctured balloon. He sank back into his chair, eyes wide, jaw hanging open, in the witness stand.

More like a witless stand, Duchet thought, replacing her glasses. She repressed a smile; she'd learned the hard way to keep her face impassive. This outcome was much more satisfying than the ridiculous notion, proposed by certain embellishers of history, of turning men into stone with a glance for no reason. Had Richard

Carter been innocent, of course, he might have stumbled over a sentence or two, but certainly would not have displayed anything on the level of this reaction.

As the judge ordered the courtroom clear of everyone but the defendant and the lawyers, Margaret Duchet made certain to be among the first to leave.

"Did I keep you waiting long, Penny?"

Margaret Duchet removed her jet-black wig as she took her seat opposite her confidant Penelope in a nearby café. Despite centuries of frequent washing and application of gels, her own hair continued to shoot out in all direction. Occasionally a few strands even peeped out from beneath the hairpiece.

It felt good to let her own head breathe, even if the London air quality left much to be desired.

"Not at all," her colleague replied. "Your timing is impeccable, as always."

"It should be. I've been doing this long enough." She reached for the menu, although she had it memorized. "I'm thinking I'll start with the grilled pigeon —"

"Madame Duchet?"

Both women looked up at the intrusive voice. A lanky, sharp-featured gentleman in a tweed coat stood beside their table.

"My apologies for the interruption," the stranger continued. "You are Madame Duchet?"

"You have the advantage of me, sir," she replied, making no attempt to keep the annoyance out of her voice. "And you are …?"

"My name is of little consequence."

"I've seen you before," Penelope put in. "Hanging about the courthouse, over the years." She turned to Duchet. "He often dresses rather oddly. Once, I recall, he entered the building as an elderly woman."

"You have a keen eye indeed, to see through my disguises," the man replied with a nod. "My closest friends and associates often cannot recognize me. I also have noticed, on at least one occasion, Madame Duchet adopting a masculine appearance. For myself, I view these impostures as an essential part of my job, with nothing odd about them. Speaking of the passage of years, I first noticed you, madam, while visiting the courthouse in my college days. That was nearly twenty years ago. Remarkably, neither of you seem to have aged a day."

"Thank you for the compliment," Duchet replied, permitting herself a thin smile. "We credit our youthful mien to the Mediterranean atmosphere of our homeland. You should visit Greece yourself one day."

"I have. I hope to spend more time there in the future. But I wonder why you attend so many murder trials. I'm not speaking just from personal observations. Some of the clerks who work at the Old Bailey tell me they frequently see you in the gallery."

Duchet dropped the smile.

She disliked intensely when people pried into her unusual life, especially behind her back. "Consider it a personal quirk of mine. I know what being murdered feels like. I find it greatly comforting to see justice served."

"Coincidentally, many of the cases you've attended ended abruptly, when, out of nowhere, the criminal admits his guilt before the entire court."

"Is that not common?" Duchet asked. "The stress of being on trial would, I expect, make it difficult for anyone to maintain a façade of innocence."

"In those penny dreadfuls, perhaps. Less so in real life, based on my own experience. Despite persuading more than one criminal to reveal his secrets myself." The stranger leaned forward. "I'm curious about your technique, Madame Duchet. How do you persuade total strangers to confess without directly interacting with them? Had you previously set things in motion, and merely attend these trials to observe the results?"

Penelope chuckled. "You make it sound as if Maggie practices some kind of ancient magic."

The man snorted. "I don't believe in the supernatural. I do, however, have many more questions. Suppose the guilty party doesn't know he is guilty? If he doesn't remember committing the crime, or remembers it incorrectly? Should he then go free? Or issue a plea of insanity?"

Duchet shook her head in disbelief. "Do you truly believe I am responsible for all those confessions?"

"Only one can attribute so much to coincidence. Knowledge of your techniques would prove invaluable in my profession, in bringing wrongs to right."

Duchet raised a hand to tap her forehead. "And that is why you ask?"

"What better reason could there—?"

The man fell suddenly silent as Duchet slipped off her emerald-tinted glasses, locking his steady gray eyes with her bright blue ones. He straightened, arms stiff, face pale, seemingly unable to even take a breath.

After a long moment, when he finally regained control of his faculties, the stranger spun and left the café without a further word, or so much as a goodbye nod.

"Well," said Penelope, with a shrug, "I suppose it's time for us to move on. Again."

Duchet waved a hand dismissively. "We've been gathering too much attention of late, in any case."

"Where shall we go this time? China?"

"I'm thinking we should revisit the Americas. We haven't been on that side of the Atlantic since it was a British colony."

"You haven't used the name Melanie since then, either."

"I don't want to go that dark. You know, the Americans recently built a bridge between two of their largest cities, both of which are on islands."

"Aye, my captain," Penelope agreed. "You've had a fondness for islands ever since the Hesperides."

"Islands and bridges. Connections are fascinating." Duchet grinned, rising. "We'll book passage at once!"

"After lunch," Penelope chided, raising a hand to signal the waitstaff.

"After lunch," her companion agreed, with just a hint of reluctance.

Margaret Duchet, by whatever name, was always up for a new adventure.

The Eyes of a Greedy Man

by Patricia Gomes

I see him looking
at her locking the door,
this man, this
greedy man
cutting the grass.
He is the landlord. Mistah
Landlord
gazing at her tanned legs, nostrils flaring,
chest puffing: "Heeeeey—
howzit goin'?"
he croons over the zzzptptpt of the mower.

"Good, everything's good." She scurries
down the path to her car.
I know what he's thinking; I've known a greedy man or two in my
time.

"Nice day, eh?" oils off his fattened tongue.
Nods and hurries with her seat belt,
blunders her key to its slot.
He
has no need to hurry.

"What, no work today?"
"Umm, no. I don't work Saturdays"
"Good for you." he purrs seductively.

Well,
seductive to him,
uncomfortable for her,
and she zips off down the road.

He stares after her—a buzzard
waiting
for the rot to set in,
waiting
for the day she's late
with the rent.
It'll happen, it always happens
with these young ones
and he'll have her then,
his greedy proclaim.
He'll have her then,
like all the rest. This is nothing new.

I gaze at the widening bald patch
on the back of his greasy head
and wonder if he knows
how fast he's losing it,
how round his gut
has gotten
these past few years,
how old
he seems to her.

Hasn't he enough?

More than he's entitled to, he has
Plenty, but to a greedy man
plenty
is never enough.
His son has a softball game today,

his daughter's dance class lets out
at two,
there's a roast in the oven for dinner,
and did you pick up the milk
on your way home?
How
does his wife, Mrs. Landlord,
amuse herself when he's gone?
Does he remember her scent/birthday/
her name?

I watch him watch her
car drive off and grin
his greedy grin, dream
his dirty dream of
grabbing
handfuls of her tempting hair
to pull her face into your crotch
and then stupidly wonder why
our pretty tresses become hissing snakes.
God save us
from
a greedy man.

Down on the Lower East Side

by Stephen Frame

There is so much that is strange here, yet so much that is familiar. Despite the strangeness, she knows this place for what it is. It is crowded like a city. It is noisy like a city. It stinks like a city. Medusa stands on the corner of Orchard and Rivington and wonders what to do.

Lisa leans in the doorway of the laundromat, draws on her cigarette and watches the woman on the corner. She has lived her whole life in New York. She knows the look of the lost when she sees it. The woman is tall, statuesque, with olive skin and braided tresses of dark hair that fall past her shoulders. Lisa stamps out her smoke and shakes her head at herself. But she has decided.

"Hey, sister, c'mon over here. Yeah, you. I'm talking to you."

The woman approaches. Lisa notices the way her braids sway as she walks. Sinuous and hypnotic, like they have a life of their own.

"You lookin' for work?" Lisa asks.

Up close, she can look the woman in the eye. The woman has beautiful eyes, Lisa thinks. But she doesn't want to hold that gaze. Not for longer than a moment.

The woman nods. "Work. Yes. I think I must work."

"It ain't much, but you can start today. Right now, if it suits you. Come on in, I'll show you what to do."

Medusa walks into the laundromat. Lisa follows, reaching out to touch the woman's hair, saying how nice it looks. Medusa turns, catching Lisa's wrist in an iron grip. "Don't," she says.

Lisa nods and says she gets it.

The laundromat is shabby, the floor speckled with soap powder. Medusa listens and watches as Lisa explains what she must do. She understands. She takes warm cloth from a place Lisa calls the drier and folds it so. The cloth smells clean and wholesome. In her head, she hears the grate of bronze swords being drawn and the screams of men dying. They scream like children. It doesn't keep them from dying.

"I gotta call Larry," Lisa says. "He owns this place. I gotta make sure it's okay for you to start, but he'll be cool with it."

"Cool with it," Medusa says.

Lisa smiles at her, dipping her head when Medusa looks her in the eye. "You're kinda goofy, you know? In a nice way."

"I am goofy," Medusa says.

Lisa bursts out laughing. "Yeah, just like that."

Medusa touches her fingers to her lips, surprised at the smile which has appeared there. In her head, the ringing of sword on shield and the pain of a honed edge meeting flesh fades a little.

"Yeah, I'll call Larry. He comes past once a week. He's okay, I suppose. He pays on time but he can be a real sleaze. Don't turn your back on him, girl. He'll find some excuse to bump into you. Jeez, it sometimes feels like he's got a snake down his pants. It's so gross."

"It would not fare well for this Larry if he touches me so."

"You got a boyfriend would come bust his chops?"

"I have no boys who are my friends," Medusa says. "I would end him myself."

Lisa gives a laugh, but it is a weak, half-hearted thing, and she looks askance at the woman whose name she has never asked. Medusa carries on working. As she works, she sings. Lisa cannot understand the words but her voice is pure and clear and Lisa starts to think she might become friends with this strange creature the city has washed up on the sidewalk outside the laundromat.

"I'll see you tomorrow then?"

"Yes. You will."

"Okay, we open up at nine. Where are you staying?"

"I have a place."

"You, uh, you never told me your name."

Medusa smiles, pleased that she can do so. "No. I did not. But I think I will."

Lisa half expects the woman not to show up the next day but she is there, waiting by the door.

"Been here long?"

Medusa shrugs. "Since dawn."

Lisa laughs and snorts. "Yeah, right."

Medusa only smiles. Later, Lisa asks her where she's from.

"Kisthene," Medusa says.

Lisa shakes her head. "Never heard of it. How'd you get here?"

Medusa hesitates before answering. "I'm not sure. There was a man. I could not defeat him. I fled. Under the earth. To here."

"Someone chased you through the subway?" But much as Lisa asks, Medusa will say nothing more. "Okay, mystery girl, you got any family?"

"I have two sisters."

"You got a boyfriend?"

"You asked me of this yesterday. No. I do not know any boys."

"I meant a man in your life." Lisa runs her fingers through her hair. "I got Frank. He's kind of my boyfriend, I think. Though he's a real jerk sometimes. Actually, most of the time. I try to dump him but he keeps coming back like a stray dog. Always sniffin' around."

"There is no man in my life," Medusa says.

Lisa takes up the challenge with some relish. "What, like never, or just recently?"

"Never."

Lisa rolls her eyes. "Yeah, right."

Medusa looks at her, with that gaze Lisa cannot hold. "I do not lie."

Lisa's hand flies to her mouth. She giggles. "A virgin in New York City in 1974? I should call *The Times*."

Medusa touches her hand to her belly. "I never said I was a virgin."

When Lisa presses her on the matter, she will say no more.

"Hey, girl, it's Saturday. What say we hit a few bars tonight and ..." Lisa looks at the woman she now thinks of as her friend. Looks closely. At the dark stains on her clothes, that might be mud or might be something else. "Where did you say your place was?"

"Not far. The space where the trees are."

"Oh my God, you're sleeping in Central Park? Are you nuts? Have you seen this?" Lisa picks up the newspaper from yesterday. "You see what it said in here? They found a dead guy in the park this week. Bitten by a snake, it says. Can you believe this city?" She puts the paper down. "Maybe you should come stay with me. Just for a few nights until we find you somewhere?"

Medusa smiles, an action she finds she enjoys very much. "I would like that."

Lisa bustles into her apartment, leading Medusa through the door. "Okay, we need to get you cleaned up. Bathroom's through there. Take off those dirty things and I'll come get them. I'm going to make some coffee."

Lisa comes back out of the kitchen and stops dead. "Uh, I meant for you to strip off in the bathroom."

Medusa stands in front of her pile of clothes. "Nakedness offends you?"

Lisa looks away and looks back. "No, I guess it doesn't." Steps closer. "What happened to you?" Reaches out to Medusa, who pulls herself back. "It's okay. I just want to see. Who did this to you?"

Medusa allows the woman to touch her, turn her gently around, finger-tips tracing the scars that stripe her body. She dips her head, breathes, enjoying the feeling of being cared for. "Men did this to me."

The apartment door opens. Lisa's head jerks round. Her voice is a strangled squeak. "Frank! Jeez, don't you ever knock?"

Frank goggles. Then smirks. "Hey, Lis, who's your new pal?"

Medusa turns to regard Frank, her arms held loose by her sides. Lisa hustles her into the bathroom. Tells her stay put. Medusa listens through the door. She does not understand when the man called Frank asks Lisa if they are queer for each other. She does understand when the man's voice drops lower and says, "Why don't we share her? Unless you want me to tell your boss he's got a dyke working for him."

Medusa pushes through the door, strides across the apartment. Frank's gaze is on her, not looking in her eyes, looking at her body. Medusa does not stop. Frank raises a hand in warning. Medusa bats it away, fastens her own hand to his throat, pins him against the wall. Looks into his eyes, shows him the merest fraction of her power.

Lisa sees. It is only a moment, a fleeting glimpse of the truth. And in all the long years she now knows she will spend with this woman, this is the only secret she will keep from her. When she sees her like this—naked, winged, and with living serpents for hair— Lisa thinks she will never see her more beautiful or more fierce.

Helpful Athena

by Sharmon Gazaway

O how you watch Medusa by the hour
as she brushes her peerless mane of inky
hair   stroke by stroke—you fairly shudder
with envy. You look at her
and she looks on and on
into the beyond of her mirror
all entwined with serpents of silver and jade—
her ringlets like living onyx
spring down past her waist
all undone.

When you curse her
and black serpents writhe
from her scalp   whispering   hissing   shining
like onyx
you watch as they coil lovingly
silkily around her fingers and wrists
living jewels that adore her ceaselessly
worship her with love-nips—
poison at the ready
to protect her if need be.
How those little deaths love her!
And she adores them—
they increase her power.
No man will ever take her again
and her garden grows

with the statuary of lovely men.
When Perseus consults you
you glance down at Medusa
and behold the writhing glory
of her reflection in the silver looking glass—

and you say
I know just the thing.

Medusa. © 2022 Matt Seff Barnes. All rights reserved.

When Lightning Strikes

by Kayla Whittle

When they finished, they looked at her and decided she was beautiful. They said to each other, *look at what we've created*, but she could not see what she had become. Lightning swam in her veins and gathered at her fingertips. In her chest, her heart beat a rhythm quickly drowned by the excited voices around her. It felt like it took an eternity—a lifetime for her, counting every minute since her heart had started—to settle into her bones and seams. Her pieces felt misaligned when she opened her eyes.

Most of the men had gone, but one had remained to watch over her. She clawed her way upright, needing no assistance, and looked at him with her new eyes. He was small, and pale, and clutched at his throat when his gaze met hers. His expression smoothed over, every angry crease easing into a smile. She felt her lips twitch in response—then he fell. She heard the breath catch in his throat, smelled the salt of his tears. Peering over the edge of her table, she watched as he twitched, but he didn't struggle. His heart slowed until it went silent.

She hadn't lived long enough to determine many things for herself, but she realized then she disliked silence.

The men returned, their voices louder, angrier. They moved too quick for her to decide if this was better than being alone. They shut out the light so she could not see them; they took the body away. They congratulated each other on their success even as they locked her away and feared being alone with what they'd built. She was given a blindfold to wear whenever they fed her or checked her seams.

At night when they left her, she lay alone and looked up toward the sky. Her room was open, bared to the sun and stars and the weather, the tumultuous weather that had given the pieces that'd lived before her new life. She decided she liked what she saw, but longed to see with her new eyes what sat beyond the edges of her piece of sky. When they returned, they said she would leave the room soon and go out into the world.

"Where will I go?" she asked, and they told her they would decide.

"What will I see?" she asked, and they told her they would show her where to look.

"You're a weapon," they said. "A beautiful one, but a weapon must be handled, and pointed in the right direction."

She thought of the man she'd seen before they covered her eyes. His face had gone so still, limbs locked and stiff. An electric tang ran through her, but the pieces that made her had been stilled, too, once. They'd known a chill finality that she didn't want to ever experience with this body they'd made for her.

The men did not ask what she wanted.

"You're ready," they told her when really it seemed they were referring to themselves.

"Tomorrow," they promised, before they left her alone, again. The door's lock sounded, loud and heavy.

She wanted to know what was on the other side of the door. In her room she had the sky, but in the stitched-together pieces of her mind she knew there was a world out there. People, like the women who'd been taken apart and reassembled into her. Her pieces remembered pushing through bustling marketplaces and speaking to rooms filled with children and rowing out onto calm, still water, tipping their faces up toward the same sun that hovered over her room.

Though she did not feel like a weapon, she thought that did not change what she had been built to be.

When they came for her, in the darkness, they hid her power behind cloth. The men guided her into the sunlight and she felt its warmth wrap tight around her in welcome. She tilted her chin upward, though the men did not like when she slowed.

"Move faster," they told her. "Don't you want to be useful? We'll allow you to see again when the time is right. You'll look, and the world will know to fear us."

She liked the sound of that, though she'd arrange the words differently.

They would fear her.

The men tried to hold her, but they had built her strong. Her hands had raised children, her arms had chopped wood, her shoulders had carried the burdens of her past. Though she knew she'd done none of it herself, she used that strength to shrug off those who would hold her back.

She lifted her blindfold and faced the world.

They fell, the men who'd made her. The ones who'd stitched together the perfect, powerful prize. Some froze, lungs and heart silent within their chests. Some cowered before her, pressing their hands against their eyes as if their flesh could keep them safe.

She left them. Her feet were bare, but they remembered climbing rocks and the feel of blistering sand. The grass folded beneath her soles and the women who made her whole sighed at the soft touch.

Standing at the crest of a hill, she saw ahead a little shorn path the men had meant to lead her down. Behind her lay the darkness, and her room, a cave, her brief glimpse into the world.

At the base of the hill lay a town filled with white buildings and dirty streets. She had never seen so many people; they might fear her new eyes, but the electricity singing in her gut didn't allow for any hesitation.

She wanted the world and she would have it. She stepped forward, blindfold in hand.

BOOK IV

Scales, Sparks, Stones

by Alexis DuBon

Hisses like newly struck matches.

Scales that glisten, that scatter light like a disco ball.

This soirée for her alone. This room bursting with statues to commemorate every man who's failed to take her.

But you won't be a statue, you'll be a legend. Immortalized through words that won't ever crumble to dust. Songs and sonnets and the glory of knowing that her story can never be told without your name as punctuation.

A symphony of hisses, an orgy of exhales as you steadily advance.

Forked tongues like licking flames.

Scales that sparkle. Eyes that burn.

You feel yourself harden.

She Who Roams Far

by Sam Muller

Not everyone is happy with my presence in this little mountain town. There are murmurs, pointed looks, even the occasional graffiti on the walls telling me to return to where I came from. But in general, I'm made to feel welcome, and assured that the justice I seek can be mine if it's rightful.

For me, that suffices.

I dress with care. It's astounding, the change in women's condition over the ages. The two partners in the law firm handling my case are women. Even the police chief is a woman, for Hecate's sake. Yet women continue to be judged by their appearance.

"Look normal," my lawyer warned me last week, over a cup of espresso.

That was another something the gods knew nothing about, coffee.

My gray suit is new and somber, maybe too somber. I drape an azure silk scarf over my shoulders and smile at my reflection in the fly-speckled mirror. I don't look like a shade out of Hades anymore.

The room phone rings. It is the receptionist. "Your ride is here, Ms. Gorgon," she says and adds, a little shyly, "I hope it goes your way."

I thank her, peek one last time at the mirror and hurry out.

The entranceway to the courthouse is packed, an ant-heap of bodies. Going in through the main door would have been impossible without a thunderbolt or two.

"The media is here in full force," the policeman driving the unmarked car tells me as he cruises past the white-painted building.

"Is it good?" I ask.

He smiles into his moustache, his dark eyes fixed on the road. "Good for us, Ms. Euryale. Until you came, we were totally off the news map. Now everyone is talking about us. Even the international press is here. We are bound to become a part of the tourist trail. Big boost to the economy, new jobs and all that, you know."

I wonder how they will sell it. Monster vs. Billionaire is the title favoured by the media. Maybe they'll just drop the billionaire part and make it all about the monster.

Still, I'm happy they are getting something out of the whole mess.

Even the rear entrance is besieged. But there is a side entrance known only to the initiated. I'm taken in through a door that looks as if it hasn't known paint since the Romans first invaded a frigid island called Britannia.

I follow the policeman up narrow stairs and narrower corridors into a little room.

"The lawyer will come for you when it's time," the policeman tells me. "Good luck, Ms. Gorgon. I hope you'll win. I really do." He pauses and adds, "I've a sister too. I'd to the same for her in your shoes if I could."

I smile my thanks, wiping my sweaty palms on the sides of my trousers.

The room has two chairs and a glass-topped table. A framed print of a tropical beach adorns one wall. The sand is white and the sea a blue that defies description. Without the palm trees, it could have been the place we called home once, eons ago.

I walk up to the window. The view is of roofs, with mountains in the distance, so majestic they make Olympus look trite.

The towering peaks remind me of Stheno, whose mountain-like strength has been turned inward ever since that terrible day.

I wept when we washed Medusa's body in spring water, buried it, raised a mound over it and planted a sapling.

Stheno never shed a tear. As I floundered in gales of grief and loss, she became my rock. I clung to her until the unbearable truth dawned on me.

My sister was turning into a rock from inside. If I didn't do something, I'll lose her too.

The oracle gave me an answer.

The head shall melt the heart.

So began my journey to find Medusa's murderer, reclaim her, bring it back to Stheno, and give her the peace she needs. A knock makes me turn. The door opens and Nelly, the senior partner of the law firm comes in with a plastic cup of coffee. "It's instant and weak, Euryale." She always gives me my full name, whatever the circumstances. "But still a kind of coffee."

I smile my thanks. If all goes as planned, I'll never be able to drink coffee again. I'll miss it. Over time, it had become my ambrosia.

I'll miss this woman too, who had become a part of my life in a time as short as the wink of an eye, a fleeting smile.

Nelly leaves. I return to the window, sipping slowly, trying to make the coffee last. What would the gods of my youth have felt had they not been gathered by time and seen these mountains?

Gods are provincial, my journey has taught me. Their vision and their holy pronouncements are hemmed in by time and geography. Divine chieftains, almighty in their little corners but clueless about the vast world beyond.

The gods who ruled my world knew nothing about ice cream or chocolate, dinosaurs or the big bang, snow or sand covered vistas. Not to mention all those other mountains that dwarf their precious Olympus, turning it into a mere hill by comparison.

The door opens. Nelly comes in. "Ready?"

I smile. Ready, yes.

For eons, I've been nothing but ready.

The courtroom is packed. All you breathe is other people. The smells barely register. My whole being is focused on just one person.

Time hasn't marked him either. He looks as well-crafted as he did that morning when he arrived in our home with his pitiful tale and his convincing manners. He was always a driven man. The outcast grandson of one king; the despised stepson of another. The unacknowledged son of a god. Perhaps it was the tangled prehistory that turned him into what he became.

A liar, a deceiver, and ultimately a murderer.

PER Seuss, Perry Seuss, he calls himself now, the owner of Seuss universities, Seuss hospitals, Seuss media and Seuss Publications.

When I arrived here, exposing him for what he was, he didn't flee or even deny my story, as he had on our previous encounters. Instead, he embraced his past.

"She who I slew was a monster," he said, "with serpentine locks that turned beholders into stone. She disobeyed the gods, resisted their will, and was punished by them. The gods sanctioned my quest. By killing her I rid the world of evil. Murder in defence of rightful order is not a crime but a necessity."

His audience cheered, hailing him as a modern-day dragon-slayer. He was offered a book deal, a movie deal, and a prominent position in a political party on the lookout for the next celebrity strongman.

That's another thing I've realized. People aren't happy unless they have enemies lurking in the wings. Anyone could fit the bill: a boatful of people fleeing war, a man who looks different, a woman who is wronged ...

In a world obsessed with monsters, monster-killers are never out of a job.

There are three judges: a woman and two men.

Nell looks at me before she gets up, a brief glance that is as full as a book. "My client wishes to make a statement," she tells the judges.

The judges confer in low voices. The spectators follow suit, but are silenced by the usher with the terrible threat of eviction from the courtroom.

A kind of silence descends. It is bereft of words, but full of sounds: clearing of throats, coughs, shuffling feet ...

The presiding judge bangs the gavel. She calls me Ms. Gorgon, and tells me to begin.

I bow.

"Honourable Judges, we were three sisters, Medusa, Stheno and Euryale, born of the sea, living amongst the waves. Gods battled in the sky and on land for overlordship; we shrugged and went on with our lives. The old gods were defeated and new gods took their place. One of them claimed all the oceans and seas as his domain. He called himself Poseidon and promised to guard and heal us. We found his words inspiring, and failed to ask why we needed to be guarded and healed.

"At first, he did nothing that warranted concern. Then we began to hear rumors, of unacceptable demands, of cruel punishments. We should have paid attention but we didn't, until the tidal wave consumed us. The protector turned predator: you know how it works. What he wanted from us we had to give, with a smile.

"Medusa refused. She refused to be a creature of that god or any god. He pursued her. She fled to the temple of the eternal virgin, believing she was safe in that holy place. But for gods, nothing is holy, outside of themselves. When Medusa pleaded for protection, the goddess turned her virginal eyes away. Still Medusa resisted, a mortal woman against a god.

"Did I tell you that of the three of us, she was the only mortal?

"She fought back and grabbed the god's tripod from him, the emblem of his authority, the pivot of his power. Bereft of his holy metal, the god fled. She threw the tripod away and returned home.

"Gods are like tides, waxing and waning. You, who never had to live under gods at the zenith of their power, cannot conceive what such a life entails. Think of the worst tyrants of your time. Imagine their potency and malignancy enhanced by a thousandfold. Then, you might be able to conceive what a god is like in his or her youth. That was what Medusa was confronted with when she sought divine justice against that rapine god.

"The gods gathered in conclave. They turned Medusa from complainant to wrongdoer, a woman who dared to raise her hand to a god. They accused her of sacrilege. When she told them what that god tried to do to her, they accused her of maligning a divinity. So the gods judged. You know what that judgment was. You have immortalized her fate in your plays, your paintings, and your statues. Her hair, her beautiful hair, was transformed, each strand a serpent. Each serpent with the power to turn any beholder into stone.

"Medusa means 'to protect.' Her worse punishment was not the ugliness. It was the loneliness. For she had to shun those she loved and who loved her. She had no other way to protect us from her petrifying gaze. She showed her face only to those who intended her harm. When they invaded her home, she defended herself. Under what law is that a crime?

"Honourable Judges, I said we were three sisters. When would-be-heroes started besieging Medusa's refuge, we became to her what she had been to us all our lives: guardians. We kept watch and we warned. Then he came, this man who stands before you.

"Perseus.

"He came as a supplicant. He said his mother, who was once raped by a god, was being held captive by a king. He wanted a lock of Medusa's serpentine hair to turn his mother's persecutor into a man-shaped rock. We believed. He went to her with our sanction. She would have been glad to help. She would have stood with her back to him and bent her head, so that he could cut one lock, one deadly snake. He cut her head off.

"We sensed her death. We rushed to her, and found her headless corpse. We washed Medusa's mangled body in spring water, arrayed it in a silken robe, and buried it. Her headless corpse is not walking the earth, crying for justice. There are no spectres in this story. The unquiet spirits belong to the living, to my sister and to me.

"I raged in my grief. Stheno's grief turned into stone. I soon had two burdens: a murdered sister and a sister who was petrifying from inside. That was when I decided to be true to my name—the far roaming one.

"I pursued this man. Time and again, I came close to him. Yet, he slipped through my fingers. This time, I trust, the outcome will be different. This man who dishonoured his word, who killed an already wronged woman not in battle, not face to face, but concealed behind a veil of lies, this man is now within the reach of justice.

"He has my sister's head. I want it.

"I told you Stheno is turning into a rock from inside. The only antidote to her slow petrifaction is Medusa's head. If Stheno can hold it in her arms, if she can lay it to rest under the earth, her grief will turn from stone into tears. *The head will melt the heart*, the oracle said. Help me save my sister. Order him to give me what is mine by kinship and love.

"That is the justice I beg from you."

It's now his turn. He will defend himself, his lawyer says. He stands up and bows, first to the judges, then to the spectators. His manner is kingly.

"Most Honourable Judges," he says, his voice rich and melodious. "I will not defend myself by lying, by insulting the pain of a bereaved sister. I will tell you my truth. I was bidden to do what I did by the gods.

"The imbalance of power between immortals and mortals is as wide as the world. That is proper. How else can gods be powerful but through the powerlessness of humans? Your Ovid quotes me in his Metamorphosis.

Medusa once had charms; to gain her love
A rival crowd of envious lovers strove
They, who have seen her, own they ne'er did trace,
More moving features in a sweeter face,
Yet above all her length of hair they own
In golden ringlets, wav'd and graceful shone.

"Yes I did say that once, or something like that. I never felt anything but pity and compassion for that wronged woman who reminded me of another wronged woman, my mother.

"You stare? Of course I knew she was no monster. The monsters were the gods who punished her for another's crime. But knowing what the gods did to the disobedient, how could I set my sense of justice against their command? How could I risk myself, risk depriving my wronged mother of her only son? In a world where might is right, the weak have no choice but to succumb.

"I can understand this woman's anger. But I'm not the guilty party here. The guilt belongs to the gods. I was merely their instrument. I wasn't acting of my own free will.

"Yes, I took Medusa's head. I didn't trust the gods. I knew how easily they could break a promise, and betray their instrument once the deed was done. So I kept Medusa's head. Armed with that weapon, even gods couldn't touch me."

"Liar," I shout. "You used my sister's head not for self-defence but for self-advancement. You used it to bargain with the gods, to gain for yourself a slice of immortality, to win a wife and a kingdom."

The judge bangs the gavel. Its sound is lost on me. He occupies my world. This is between us, as it always was.

"Give me Medusa's head," I tell him. "Then you can go your way, free of me."

He holds out both hands, helpless, appealing, regretful. Deceptive. "I wish I could. But it's beyond my power. Medusa was mortal. Her head went the way of all mortal things."

He pauses, looking me straight in the eye. "I assure you, I gave it a decent burial."

"Where did you bury it?" I ask him.

"I can't remember," he answers.

"You will tell me, even if I have to chase you for endless eons," I tell him.

He bows. I catch the glimmer of a smile in his eyes.

Words desert me. Around me I hear the buzz of conversations, the bang of the gravel, the stentorian voice of a judge demanding silence …

I'm on my own track. I pursue that smile to its origin. Then I know. It fits with the fate of the gods, not dead, but faded into oblivion. It explains why he and I remain outside of time, of history.

The knowledge is shattering. Still, I have no choice but to accept it.

I turn away from him, toward the judges. "Your Honour, I withdraw my complaint."

The court descends into tumult.

He stares at me, the gold-flecked eyes wide, the prefect mouth open revealing pearly white teeth. Even gods didn't have such white teeth. Dentistry was probably another thing they knew nothing about.

"Why?" he shouts.

"You have nothing I want," I tell him.

His smile is back. A honey-pot to a fly. "I do. You want to know where Medusa's head is. Who else can answer that question but me? Come, together we will search for it. I will …"

I turn away from him. I bow to the judges, and to the courtroom.

"I wasted your valuable time," I tell them. "I imposed on your patience. For that, I owe you an apology and an explanation.

"The gods who ruled the world in the time we were young have diminished into myths because no one believes in them anymore. This man and I are unchanged from what we were because of my hatred of him, and his fear of me. Hate and fear create and sustain belief. You can't hate what you don't believe in; you can't fear what you don't believe in.

"So, I lay aside my hate and end my quest. I am now free to go. I hope he is too."

As I leave, the court erupts. His voice soars above all other noises.

"Euryale, wait, Wait, WAIT!"

I'm in the car again, a different car. Nelly drives it. "Where can I take you?" she asks.

"The edge of the town would do," I say.

She stops at a lonely spot, the looming mountains forming a backdrop. We get down. I hold out my hand. "Thank you for everything."

She takes my hand. "I won't pretend to understand all of what happened. But I feel it was a good ending for you."

I pull her into an embrace. "It will be, when oblivion claims us."

She raises an eyebrow. "Oblivion is good?"

Good? I ponder. "It is the only thing that makes eternity bearable."

I walk up the path leading to the mountains. At the bend I turn around. She waves. I wave back.

Stheno sits under the trees, more motionless than the trees.

I sit next to her, hold her hand in mine. Her fingers return my clasp, barely.

We say nothing. Neither of us. We sit silently in a world of sounds—waves, leaves, wind, birds—I hear them all.

The light fades. Sunlight, moonlight, starlight. Silence creeps in, washing out all noise.

Before the silence is complete, I hear a voice calling my name. And Stheno's. I know whose voice that is, or I could know it, if I want to. But I don't want to.

I want nothing now.

Or maybe just the one thing.

As the last grain of light melts, together with the last whispered rustle, she comes.

And we sit, the three together again, as nothing embraces everything.

Jellyfish

by Avra Margariti

Hers is not a head of hissing
snakes but of snapping suckers,
each tentacle frilly and baroque.
The ocean's brogue, a siren susurration
hazy as the dawn above, a mauvish bruise
the like of Athena's callous mercy: a thumb
denting Medusa's jellyfish form.

(*Aren't you glad*, the goddess said,
that I hid you right under Poseidon's nose,
floating through his aquatic kingdom

where he'd never think to look for you?)

One look now and she turns ships
into wrecks and hearts into flotsam.
Dull sand transmuted: nacreous mothers,
daughter pearls.
And the stone statues of cruel
kings erected in stone, once-exiled
to the sea in their unwieldy likeness,
now coming to flesh-and-blood life.
They burble royal bubbles
of repentance in the shape of her name
as they swim duly to shore.

And the mermaid figureheads
of worn wood, Medusa's gaze unmakes
them too in her unorthodox curse.
They swim around her, a seafoam-skinned
shoal immune to her potent power
after the first sting of it, toxin-induced.
A sea of burning metamorphoses
to join the eternal undertow.

Excerpt from The Snakes We Feed

by Christina Bagni

"Medusa?" Helen stopped singing, reached for her pen in her boot. "This is like, a breakup song, right?"

I tilted my head, started over toward her. "No, it's—"

"Are you alright?" she cut in.

I cleared my throat, shook my head. "Yeah. No worries."

I stood beside her and glanced over the lyrics. I could smell her: peaches and coconut, honey and tree bark. She smelled the same as she had since I'd known her.

"I guess it could be. It was just an angry song, before. But it could work as a breakup song."

"Well, hey, if it's an angry song it can be an angry song. I just —"

"No," I insisted, backing away from the paper and playing a few random notes on my electric lyre. "I like the idea."

I smiled and she smiled warily in return and started scribbling on the paper. "What about, 'I've cried fifteen rivers since you stopped being mine,' then?"

"That's good," Paris said from the stands. "I like it."

"Wait," Achilles said with a laugh in his voice. "So, if it's a breakup song, now 'take me down' is …"

"Uh oh," Helen said, a wide, goofy smile spreading on her face. "'Take me down,' baby! Is that too sexual for Mr. Strabo?"

Mr. Strabo was the random history teacher who was the supervisor for the talent show and technically ran the whole thing, though mostly he just shut various dance groups down for being too sexy.

"Pretty sure literally any song is toeing the line," Achilles snarked back, and a smile actually played at his lips.

I smiled too, surprising myself again at how quickly my bitterness evaporated. Her adjustment was cool, and I was impatient to hear her sing it. A few more things to do first— Achilles and I worked out a chord structure, and I figured out a nice descant and solo to bridge together the chorus and verse. Pat kept it basic for now, just tapping the high hat to keep us in time as Helen started at the top.

She sang the first few lines of the verse I wrote, a pulsing rhythm I didn't realize could be so darkly sexual. She twirled her hair with her free fingers, putting on a show for Paris, who was doing homework and watching us practice from the back of the music room. He bobbed his head and pointed playfully back at her when she pop-star pointed at him. Pat threw in a break and the bass and Achilles and I got louder to match him. It forced a smile to my face. Hell yeah. Now this is getting somewhere.

Then Helen turned to me, still playing the part, sauntering up and stomping her foot to the beat. She looked me right in the eye and sang, "*I want to feel your knuckles between me and the ground,*" which I'd written as an angry line, a violent line. But when she sang it with a pout, with her eyes peering up at me from under her thick eyelashes, I saw her, beneath me, pinning my hands to the floor, her eyes half-closed and her lips half-open, the weight of her against the back of my fingers and I fumbled on my lyre and made a terrible feedback noise on the amp, which made everyone laugh and stop playing.

I forced myself to laugh too, but was mortified, and played it off like I did it on purpose, fanning myself and acting flustered and so on until Helen took it from the top again, taking it more seriously this time.

Pat came in from the top with the snare and the bass and I caught my breath, chastising myself in my mind, just trying to get through this so I could curl up on my bed and hopefully stop breathing.

She made it through the full verse this time, and we stumbled through the chorus Helen wrote, and we didn't sound all that terrible—Pat kicked up the tempo and Helen really belted out those lines, throwing in some on-purpose voice cracks like she always does.

"Maybe it's not a ballad after all," Achilles said and nudged me with his elbow. I wasn't expecting it and leapt away, gasping, my mind clashing with Helen beneath me and Perseus on top of me and hissing and ocean and salt and pain. I pressed my fingers into the strings until they pressed past my calluses.

"Sorry," Achilles said.

"It's okay." Under my breath. Needed to get out of here. Pulled the strap up over my head, rested the lyre against the stands, headed to the door, the lyre slipped and hit the ground, blaring noise into the amp. Helen ran over to rest her hand on the strings.

I told them I was going to the bathroom. I ran down the hall, certain I was going to throw up. I slammed the doors behind me and cried in the stall for like a full minute. Tried to push through the sadness as absolutely quickly as possible. Stared at the rust in the bottom of the sink, watched my stomach and chest heave with every breath. Stared at my skinny red knuckles, *definitely* shaking, numb hands. Stared at myself in the mirror. I wanted to fall into the blackness of my eyes.

I couldn't feel this way for long without telling myself I was being overdramatic, and then arguing with myself over whether I was being honest about my own feelings, or if I was exaggerating, or if I was just being dramatic, or if all of this, everything I was feeling was real. I couldn't fucking tell anymore.

I was wearing a hat. I never wear hats. Everyone noticed. It was woolen and hot. It was ugly as fuck. One braid curled out the bottom and rested on my shoulder. The top of the beanie was still for a moment, then, as if it knew I was watching, moved, slowly, swellingly, like a very pregnant woman's belly. I grabbed the top of my hat and whipped it off.

Some of my dark hair frizzed with the static, making a crinkly, faint halo. And there, starting just an inch or so behind and above my temple—where my horns would go, I thought, with a scoff—was the rounded, scaly muscle of the bottom of a snake. It flexed and picked itself up from where it was nesting in the hammocked beanie bottom at the nape of my neck. It hovered up and over to lick at the air before me, to examine the mirror, then finally to get as close to my face as my mom gets to her phone when she doesn't feel like finding her glasses. My reddening knuckles gripped the edge of the sink and a fistful of beanie tighter. I breathed shallowly through my nose and resisted the urge to swat at the snake like a bee.

Its tongue flickered and almost touched me. My heart started thrumming in my ears.

I could feel the ends of its muscles moving in me, like a fetus, like a parasite, like a tumor with tentacles, terrifyingly close to my brain. The thing wormed closer to me, dark brown, scaly, solid, real, impossible, and feathered its tongue under my eyes. It lapped up my tear. I made a small noise when I exhaled, a stifled moan of fear and disgust I tried hard to keep inside.

It twisted its way back up. I winced when its movement pulled at the scabs I had made trying to tear it off my skull when it had first appeared.

I have to tell someone.

But I know that once I do ...

Maybe it will just go away.

Better to just not. Right after—right after the party, after he attacked me, raped me on the beach, I missed my period. I freaked out for a month, checking every sign, taking multiple tests I didn't believe, and eventually, it was all okay. If I had told someone, it would have been a whole—*thing*. I told everyone about the attack. That's enough drama as it is.

I'd have honestly rather died than made Helen treat me like even more of a victim. I pulled the beanie back over my ears and stuffed in the bits of hair that stubbornly poked out, and continued to poke out, pulled by the sweat on the very fingertips that fought to keep them in the hat.

I'll figure it out.

"I'll figure it out," I told my reflection. I nodded. I looked like I didn't believe myself.

Maybe it'll just … work itself out. Just go away.

Maybe it'll just kill me. Two birds with one stone.

Just kidding. Mostly.

Maybe it'll never go away.

I left the bathroom before the panic could take me over.

Fuck. Fuck. Fuck. Fuck. I chanted it to the rhythm of my footsteps.

Don't Tell Me to Smile

by Kristin Cleaveland

"Welcome," the cashier calls with a minor note of irritation in her voice, as I walk through the sliding doors just before closing time. I lift a hand in her general direction, but don't turn my head to face her. Picking up a shopping basket from the stack by the doors, I head toward the nail polish display instead. The bright, glossy colors appear dull through the dark lenses of the large sunglasses I wear to obscure the top half of my face, while a disposable mask covers the bottom. I select a bottle and hold it up to the light, squinting as I turn it. In my head, I picture it as a dark, glossy serpentine green, but I've been disappointed before. I drop it into my basket anyway and walk further into the store.

This drugstore—only blocks from my house—is one of the few places I dare venture, now that the mask has offered me anonymity.

Despite my happiness at being out in the world, I still can't leave home without feeling guilty about the unfortunate circumstances that finally offered me a taste of freedom. I have nothing to fear from a virus, but I wear the mask always, along with the sunglasses. For the first time in years uncounted, I can leave the shelter of my home and still avoid being perceived.

I love the drugstore and all it contains: the cheap candy at the checkout counter; the fragrant rows of shampoo I sniff but never buy; the brightly colored cosmetics, each promising more miraculous results than the last. I have likely tried more beauty remedies than any woman on earth—everything from bathing in donkey's milk, covering my lips in crushed carnelian beetles, and painting my knees with colorful designs. I purchase all the latest products, even though no one sees the results but me.

After all these years, I still admire myself in the mirror. My face remains unlined, my complexion unchanged. I don't need sheet masks and moisturizers and tiny pots of eye cream, but I buy them anyway. It makes me feel more connected to the women I see in the aisles, in the magazines, on Instagram. I am not one of them, but some days, I almost believe.

My scalp itches and I fight the urge to reach under the knit beanie I'm wearing. I pat it instead, stroking my hair lightly over the cap. I make a shushing sound under my breath. Momentarily distracted, I don't notice a man standing in the main aisle, scrolling on his phone. He's the one blocking the way, but I'm the one who murmurs an apology as I try to squeeze past him. He looks up from his phone.

"That's all right, sweetheart," he says. "How're you today?"

I ignore him and keep walking, until he steps in front of me, blocking the aisle.

"Why you in such a hurry? Can't say hello?"

"I really need to get moving," I say, trying to keep my voice light. I manage to move past him and head to the cooler on the wall for a bottle of water. His footsteps echo behind me.

"Why you got those big glasses on? And a mask, too. Silly," he says, and reaches for a can of Monster. "Why don't you take that thing off? Stop living in fear."

I know I should let it go, just nod in his direction, maybe, and walk away. But I'm so tired of men like him, never content to leave women alone, always offering unsolicited advice and unwanted opinions.

"I'm not afraid," I say, taking a bottle of water from the cooler and putting it in my basket. "Maybe you should be, though. Sometimes people think they're brave, but actually, they're just foolish. They don't see the danger right in front of them."

The man's laugh is a sharp and brutal sound. "Only danger I see is from people like you, trying to take away freedom from people like me." He leans in closer, but I stand my ground. I know this isn't about freedom, or fear, or anything except control. I can feel the animosity radiating from this man, and although he says he's not afraid, I know he's lying, because I can smell fear in a way that most cannot. He may be able to fool himself, but he can't fool me.

"You oughta take that mask off, maybe you'd smile more. I bet you got a pretty smile." His breath is sour, even through my mask.

"Stand back," I tell him. "This conversation is over."

"Oh, I don't think so," he replies, leaning even further in. "I wanna see that smile."

My scalp is itching even more now, and I smooth my hand over my beanie again. "No, you don't," I reply. "I'm warning you."

I turn to go, partly hoping he'll leave me alone, but also partly wishing he'll persist until he learns "no" the hard way.

Before I can take a step, he catches me by the elbow.

I turn to face him again, see the smirk on his face, see the premature triumph in his eyes as he snatches the thin paper mask from my face, crumples it up in his palm, and throws it to the floor.

He watches my face to see if I'll cry, or scream, or perhaps even apologize. But I don't. I smile, pulling my ruby-red lips slowly away from my brilliant white teeth, far enough that he can see the sharp, elongated incisors. I drag my tongue across my teeth, feeling a drop of cool blood well to the surface. Through the dark glasses of my lenses, I see the fear that he can't deny anymore.

For the first time since our brief encounter, the man is silent. I think about turning my back again, walking away. Maybe it would be enough to make him think twice before putting his hands on a woman. Maybe he'd learn from the experience, realize he doesn't know everything, figure out when to leave well enough alone. But thousands of years of life on this earth have taught me that's unlikely.

I glance around the aisles to see if anyone else is in sight, but people have given the man and me a wide berth, not wanting to get involved. For a moment—the briefest moment—I push my sunglasses on top of my head. My hair squirms in response, and the glasses fall back onto my nose almost immediately. But it was long enough.

I leave the basket in the aisle and dart toward the exit, before he is found, before I can hear the screaming and the shocked exclamations begin. I feel a bit of sorrow knowing I'll never come back to this drugstore, the tiny haven of quiet comfort I'd known for a brief time. Soon I'll be moving on again, to a new home, with a new name—though my true name, known only to myself, remains eternal. The hissing under my hat is louder, and the itch frantic, until I'm in my car, screeching out of the parking lot. I yank my hat off and set the serpents free.

Love Bites

by Eric J. Guignard

It is known that Medusa bore heirs, and those heirs begat their own progeny, so that such descendancy has continued through present-day.

Like all offspring, the genetic traits passed down through mating are mixed, altered, slivers of replicates of those who came before. And, like now, or ten thousand years ago, we change, we evolve, yet are the same, comingling with banshees, with nymphs, with myth and shadow, with gods and mortals and more.

So you whisper longing into the ear of today's lover, and hear a rustle in return: Watch out for that last remaining viper in their hair.

Firsts

by Marshall J. Moore

All men want to believe they are a woman's first.

First kiss, first love, first fuck. The first to claim, to conquer. For that is what we are to them: not people, but territory awaiting a staked flag, ready to be plundered. They claim no interest in those of us already explored by another, yet that lie is as transparent as their intentions. Each thinks, in his hubris, that he is uniquely gifted by the gods, that he can restore virginity through sheer prowess, so that he may reclaim it for himself. As though his puny little instrument could rewind time itself.

But there is no power in this world or the next that can undo the past, no matter how we may wish for it.

The man following me home is not the first to do so, not even close. He has no idea how many of his predecessors have stalked after me under these flickering streetlights, lumbering clumsily through the night.

Like the others, he does not even bother to keep to the shadows. He walks openly, brazenly, his heavy footfalls echoing off the brownstones and fire escapes. In his confidence he dares any Samaritan to intervene. None do, and his passage remains unchallenged. He does not know whether I have noticed his pursuit, and would not care either way. Perhaps it might even thrill him, to scent my fear like a hunting wolf. Like most predators, he and his kind are prowling, opportunistic creatures.

He has followed me since the bar, but his eyes have clung leechlike to me all night. He first attempted gallantry; the age-old tradition of offering to buy me a drink. How quickly that mask crumbled at my refusal. As though I have never been called an ugly bitch before. But then, all men want to believe they are a woman's first.

They are all alike, and just as easy to read. He thinks maybe once he has me alone, I will change my mind, as though privacy could somehow make him more appealing. As though getting me alone were not the entire point.

Like all of them he is bigger than me, taller, likely stronger. That is what it comes down to, really. Strength. Men are weak. Only in hurting do they feel strong. Only in taking do they feel whole. It would almost be enough to pity them, were I not the one taken.

Once, I remind myself as I turn the corner onto my street. My hands are shaking, as they always do. Only once, and never again.

I catch a glimpse of my reflection in the darkened windows lining the street, though mercifully it is distorted and vague. The man following me was not wrong in calling me ugly. The scars on my scalp are mostly covered by a wig, but those on my face cannot be hidden.

Nor do I see any reason to hide them. I wear them openly, defiantly. The message they declare to the world is twofold. To the one who gave them to me, they are a declaration that I survived. That even with all he took from me, he could not break me.

That one day, he will know what it feels like to be powerless and afraid.

To those like him they are a warning, as clear and unsubtle as the telltale patterning of a venomous snake. They say that I have endured worse pains and greater horrors than any they might inflict. That I am inured to their cruelties. That I am more a monster than they could ever aspire to be.

My scars should discourage them, should make them think twice about eyeing me, touching me, following me. And sometimes, they do. Sometimes they slink away, chastened, ashamed at the glimpse I offer into their own depravity.

But not always.

There are always a few who take those scars as a challenge. There is something they find arousing about my ugliness. An invitation to prove that no woman can resist them, whether they choose charm or force. In their arrogance they assume that someone as hideous as me should be grateful to them for deigning to offer the gift of their pleasure. My inevitable refusal compounds their rage with the humiliation of slighted pride.

That then is why they follow me. Not out of desire, or for the stoking of their ego my conquest might provide, but to revenge themselves for being denied. To punish me for my ugliness, for my willfulness. For daring to say no.

At least, that is their intent. They cannot hurt me any longer. Not in any way that matters.

My keys jangle in my hand as I turn from the street, just as they shook on that first night. Now as then, fear wraps its cold fingers tight about my spine, reminding me that the safety of the home is an illusory one.

That fear lends me speed, my heels beating out a staccato *tap-tap* as I cover the long stone path leading from my street to my front steps. My steps are watched by the silent statue sentinels that litter my garden, each one with his face contorted into a rictus of horror. At first there were only one or two, but over the years my collection has grown into a veritable throng.

At least my neighbors are not the sort to complain.

I ascend the steps to my front porch, keys in hand. In the glass reflection of the front door, I see my stalker hesitating at the edge of my garden, doubt creeping in now that the moment of action is at hand. Not doubt in his ability—he would never even consider the possibility that he may not be able to overpower me—but the faint whisper of conscience still tugging at his breast, the desperate moral voice pleading with him not to delve further into his own wickedness.

I wait with serpentine patience, slowly removing the contact lenses from my eyes. There is time yet for him to repent, though I have as little faith in him as I do in gods.

The man makes his choice, crossing his moral Rubicon and the boundary line of my property in the same step. I watch his reflection approach in the window, his long strides purposeful as he closes the distance between us.

This close to the glass, I cannot avoid my own reflection. It smiles at me, revealing a monster as terrible as the one marching up my garden path. There is no difference between he and I, save one.

I did not choose to be what I am.

He is nearly to the porch when I finally turn, facing him for the first time since the bar. Surprise makes his steps falter, wary of this sudden change. It is one thing to ambush prey unsuspecting, another to corner her in her lair.

I smile at him, revealing teeth that were once shattered by a fist. He flinches but does not stop, his feet ascending the first step to my porch as I pull the wig from my head, revealing the writhing coils of scar tissue that cover my scalp. His jaw falls open in stupefied horror, his eyes rising unwillingly to mine. In them I see the reflection of my slit pupils, my yellowed irises. Yet my gaze holds no danger for myself.

A shudder courses through me, crawling from my tailbone up my vertebrae, building in strength like a mounting wave. The sensation is both painful and pleasurable, and by the time it reaches the place behind my eyes I can barely hold it in.

The man makes a sound; a gurgle that dies before it can become a full-throated scream. His terror is enough to push me over the edge, and I release the power I am holding.

I watch, still smiling my venomous smile, as his flesh begins to calcify. It starts at the extremities, his fingers hardening into white stone. Veins of marble crawl up his arms, spreading across his body like an infection. The flesh between them stiffens until it too is white stone, pure as his soul is not.

He is truly screaming now, but it is voiceless, his throat already closing off as the marble veins crawl up his jaw. His eyes are the last to go, reflecting loathing and fear back at me until they abruptly become stone-blank.

It is over.

I sink into myself, exhausted. Each time wearies me, and not only in body. Each statue added to my collection erodes another tiny piece of my soul. I wonder how many more it will be until there is nothing left of the woman I once was, and only the monster remains.

The statue before me, once a man, was not my first.

Nor will he be my last.

Set in Stone

by Owl Goingback

You come slithering into my virtual den,
like the serpents that crown me,
bearing your sword of lies,
eyes hungry with desire.

I see the shadow of Poseidon upon you
and know you bring rape, and not love,
seek only conquest of the flesh,
not desires of the heart.

But I bid you welcome,
whispering promises of erotic sensations
in exchange for electronic silver.
If only you follow me, if only you swipe right.

Your eyes grow wide as my dance begins.
My clothing falls away in delicate layers
revealing porcelain skin beneath,
my face and eyes obscured by strategic shadows.

You move closer, breathing heavy,
your image growing larger on the screen.
Memories of long ago fill my mind.
"Is that you, Perseus?"

I touch myself
and moan with desire.
Run fingers through my hair
and awaken the vipers.

You beg to see all of me,
and I let the shadows fall away
revealing the wrath of Athena.
Horrific visage, assassin's gaze.

I watch as the lust freezes on your face,
a moment set in stone, as you become
a forever statue for someone's garden.
A gift from a modern Medusa.

Monstrous Birth

by Renée Meloche

I took the name Medusa, so the world would know me for what I had become. The guardian—protector of these cliffs, these dark woods. This world that relegates its monsters to the dark corners. The ruler of my will, my desire, my fate. The sinuous, twining quality of my nature apparent for all to see—from *she* to slithering *they*.

See the girl I once was. She is young, yet. Her body in the first bloom of youth, her skin bronzed and her legs strong from countless hours spent scaling the sheer cliffs of her island. Her black eyes are bright and curious, her smile easy, flashing strong teeth. Her hair curls in dark, inviting tendrils around her collarbone, the well-fed swell of her cheeks. She makes her small offerings in the village temple to wise and shining Athena.

She watches her father's flock, from her favourite perch atop the largest boulder in the rock-strewn pasture. The sheep bleat, calling to her, the sound of their hooves muffled by the dew-drenched grass along the cliff's edge. The breadth of the pasture stretches out beneath her, down to the dark ocean lapping at the shore. She holds the entire island in her gaze. The wind singing through the distant oaks, the great exhalation of the sea, speak to the girl of home. She would gather every rock, every tree, every creature scaled or hooved if she could, and cradle them to her breast, preserving them in the morning's stillness forever.

Her eyes—once mine—catch the glint of gold from the shore.

She slips from her perch. The joyful whinnying of horses echoes up from the beach, carried to her on the back of the warming, rising air, and she creeps to the edge of the cliff. Her eyes grow wide at the sight of a man's bare skin, glinting in the morning light, the beard on his dark face thick and curling. His broad hands are splayed against slowly-turning sky, the indigo stain of night yielding to the blushing pink touch of dawn.

Where before there was only an empty stretch of sand, the god —for that is what he is, as I will come to learn—beckons hoof and flank forth from salt-spray. Horses break from the surf, fully formed, filled with life. They bound onto the beach, bodies glistening with saltwater, powerful muscles and slick hides limned in the buttery light of the rising sun.

I knew the stories, even then, of monsters who rose up out of the earth with fangs and teeth bared, facing heroes with shining swords, men of legend. I knew what the poems said about those gods-touched men—and what they said of the women, the cursed girls who drew the eyes and ire of the gods down from the broad sky, out of the depths of the ocean. I knew.

And still, I wanted. A yawning chasm opened inside of me, reaching for him. In memories, now, I steal down and meet the god that first day on the beach, and I ask him—*what is it like to walk through the world with such power?*

See the girl I once was. She slips away from the cliff's edge, back to her flock, unseen.

We met again, the god and I, by the same beach, at the steps of the temple to Athena. Stories speak still of how he took me there, against my will. Does the will of a girl really mean so little? History remembers only the victors. It was my desire that won his favour that night. My will that won my freedom.

See the girl, the length of so many days written on her sun-burnished skin. She is older now, and the men who have come from across the sea to settle in her small village, to push beyond its borders, begin to notice her. She stays close to her father's flock, grazing them in pastures high in the hills, skirting the sky-piercing oaks and shrubs of thick, flowering myrtle. The men call out to her from their fields, where they lash the island's wild horses to their plows; from the yawning cracks in the cliffside where they mine ore, copper and, most precious of all, gold, like the ichor flowing through the gods' veins. They see the bloom of the girl's breast, the curve of her waist, the flash of her eyes, and they reach for her with leering smiles and bristling teeth.

Her father speaks to her of life beyond their island. The men are leaving, he says. They have exhausted the meagre mine. Their crops have withered and died in the arid soil. They will cross the sea again, seek their fortunes elsewhere.

"You will go with them," her father says. "They have paid me a fair price in gold."

"I will not," says the girl, and though her heart slams in her chest, her voice is strong. "This is my home, and I belong to myself. No man may take me against my will."

"The only will that matters, *kore*, is the gods'," says her father. "And the only name, the one that you will take from your husband. A child who disobeys her father is a monstrous thing. It will lead only to ruin."

The girl's face heats, cold washing over her like a second skin. No thing could be so monstrous as a father discarding his child to the callous desire of men, the cold will of the gods.

I stole out of my father's house that night, down to the beach, scrambling over the scrim of the ocean cliffs. The swollen moon hung low in the black sky, calling the ocean up to the shore. I drew off my chiton, leaving it crumpled in a pile on the temple steps.

See the girl in the wine-dark ocean. The water is colder than she expects, yet it yields to her, forming around the swells and dips of her body, snaking gently through the coils of her hair.

When the god finally appears, the girl goes to him, slicking cool water like silk through her trembling fingers. His eyes reflect starlight from unimaginable depths, and his golden hands are strong and warm around her waist as he pulls her toward the shore.

The god leads her to the quiet shelter of a cave near the beach. There, they lay down upon the damp sand, and his hands roam across the girl's feverish skin, tangle in her long, dark tresses, splay clever fingers over her strong legs. The weight of their desire will crush her, if the girl does not surrender. She gives herself over to it, to the salt air and night sky, to that sweet and painful pleasure.

The god tells her his name is Poseidon.

The girl asks him if he knows her fate.

Poseidon face is still, inscrutable. "What a strange thing you are," he tells the girl. "No mortal knows their own fate. It is whatever the gods will."

The girl is persistent. "I wish to know if there is room enough in the world for more than just the will of gods," she says.

The god frowns, his clever fingers pulling at the fullness of his beard. "I see. And do you think, *kore*, that the worm, desiring the power of a python, should have it?"

The girl pushes up to her elbows, eyes flashing.

Poseidon's laughter booms, echoes off the cave walls, breaks over her like a slow-rolling wave. "Calm now, *kore*! The world is shaped by the will of the gods, but so too by desires of men. What a monstrous thing, desire." The god's ivory smile glints in the gloom, his voice low like the first murmuring of a storm blowing in from sea. "Would you like me to show you?"

The girl leaps upon him, her strong legs binding his waist, wet sand shifting underneath them on the cavern floor. She grips his clever fingers with her rough, work-coarsened hands. She brings her mouth to his sweat-covered skin, drags her lips across the most sensitive parts, and shows him just how monstrous, how glorious, the desire of a girl can be.

When they have finished, the girl speaks again.

"The gods shape the world and subject men to their will. I am not a man, but I too desire to shape the world. This island is my home. My desire is to preserve it, shelter it from a world that would strip from it anything it can, the men that will leave it bare and wanting. I wish to protect that which I hold dear."

"Desire can a monstrous thing," the god says again. "A foul thing, like a creature born in the dark without limbs, scaled and crawling."

"But why should it be so?" the girl asks. Inside her, the yawning chasm of desire stirs. It twines around her will, coiled, sharp and lovely. Waiting.

The god looks down at her, his wine-dark eyes brimming with a hunger not yet sated. "Speak to me once more of a girl's desire," he says.

And the girl smiles, her teeth flashing white and sharp under the swollen moon. Ready.

The god sighs as his body sinks into hers once more, and as the white foam of the tide crawls steadily toward them, the girl sinks her teeth into the burnished column of his neck, the golden glow pulsing underneath his skin. It is enough to make him groan, deep and loud, shaking the earth. Enough to draw forth his pleasure and hers, the smallest bead of god-gold ichor, trailing a path of acid pain and desire across her darting tongue.

I left the god to his sated sleep and stole into the dark, cool of the temple. There I called out to my goddess, Athena. My patron goddess knew something of the desire of men, the will of gods, the pain of self-birth, the monstrous nature of desire.

She asked me what I wanted, and I repeated the petition that had fallen on her brother's lust-deafened ears.

My goddess reshaped me. Under her *aegis*, I was now the guardian of my island. The glowing taste of ichor I had stolen from Poseidon hummed within me, singing of flesh and stone. I took the name Medusa, so that the world, should it seek me out, would know who I was.

See Medusa stalk the cliffside caves and deep woods of their island home, crowned with the scaled and seething lemniscate of serpentine bodies, bright dark eyes, flickering tongues. They haunt the rocky outcrops with the flash of their yellow eyes and the rustle of their scales over stone. They part a thorny shrub and return a fallen fledgling to their mother's nest. They keep the sheep from straying into the dark, grasping heart of the oak forest. They perch atop the boulders in the rock-strewn pastures, watching, holding the sweep of the island from field to shore in their gaze.

At first, the men of the village are brave. They bring their rakes and their forks and even one dull, rusted sword into Medusa's domain. The sound of Medusa's laughter is thick with venom. They rend the men limb from limb, throwing the remains from the cliffs, chumming the water for the fish and serpents in the sea below.

They spare only one man from the village. "I am Medusa," they tell him, flashing their bristling teeth in a leering, hundred-headed smile. "Go, and tell all those you encounter my name."

The knowledge passes far beyond the boundaries of their island. Many more travel to Medusa's well-tended coast, flocks of sailcloth and flashing bronze where they make landfall in their vessels of glory and war. Heroes chancing to kill one of the new monsters of this age. They are the last to perceive how the glory of a girl's desire and her will, the monstrousness of her nature, intertwine.

I grew older, and as I did, I wished to know more.

Poseidon visited me still, though less often, tangling his thick fingers in the seething mass of my hair, whispering into the delicate, scaled shell of my ear. The hunger in my eyes recognized the hunger in his.

I asked the god to teach me the song of stone, and he could not refuse me.

I learned, too, of the world beyond the edge of my island's shores. How it came to pass from the golden age of the gods-touched heroes who conquered lands undreamt of with blazing courage and burnished copper, into the diminished glory of kings and their armies, riven by greed and gold.

"Soon there will be no true heroes left," Poseidon lamented. "Then, too, will the age of gods and monsters end."

Under the god's instruction, I had learned something more of men, how their bodies were flesh made of air and salt and water. Heroes journeyed to my island and, rather than send them back to their inglorious world battle-spent and venom-wracked, I kept them. From salt and air and water, I remade men into stone; heroes preserved at the height of their glory, forever.

"You will draw the ire of men this way, little snake," said Poseidon, teasing my serpentine tresses, when he saw the gallery of statues I had spun from heroes and stone.

"Teach me to craft creatures from the sea and air, and I will end this little game," I countered. I had not forgotten the way he had looked that day, gold-limned hands splayed across the air, beckoning horses forth from the spray of ocean surf.

"The game will end whether or not you will it," said the god, his countenance somber. "And gods and monsters will be forgotten."

"Then I will make my own legacy," I said. "I will make them see me, in every song that is sung in this age, and the next. In every story that is told. In every girl who might have once been favoured—or cursed—by the gods."

Poseidon's eyes flashed. "And how will you accomplish such a thing?"

"By the will of the gods," I said.

I would not rest until I could bring something of my own design, out of the sun and salt and water, into this earth.

See Medusa there, on the brilliant, glaring white of the island shore, the wind sharp and the sun bearing down on the day the last of the age's great heroes appears.

His sharp, dark silhouette looms across the mouth of the cave where they had once lain with Poseidon. The boy—for that is what he is—flashes with armor so reflective, Medusa startles at the sight of their many selves made duplicate, thrown into sharp relief.

They come to the mouth of the cave to greet him.

"Medusa!" he cries. "You have laid waste to the noble men of this country. Atone for your crimes!"

See the multiplicities of forked tongues that pierce the air. Medusa approaches, the scales of their belly scraping across the stone steps of the small temple to Athena.

"I have nothing to atone for," they say. Their face is smooth and unblemished after all these years spent dwelling in the dark of their forests and their caves. It cracks into a smile that glints like the edge of a blade. "There was once room enough in the world for us all."

The boy avoids Medusa's gaze.

His voice is low and frightened. "You will not corrupt my will, monster. There is not room enough in this world for us both."

See Medusa's serpentine crown cease its twisting movements. It is true. Every day, this world becomes less like the one they swore to protect. They are growing older, and as the sun has passed across the sky, the tides have come in and slipped back out again, the rust has withered the blades and spears littering the beach, so too has their desire waned.

I was ready, the day the boy came with his over-polished, ill-fitting armour.

In the ages I have lived, I had learned all I could about the desires of men and the will of the gods. I had seen enough of the world, enough of the swords and the greedy, grasping hands of men. Hadn't someone once told me that disobeying the will of the gods would lead to ruin? I had lived more than my fair share of life, avoiding ruin, and now my fate had come to meet me, and I would greet it as an old friend, leaving one last offering to my patron, my goddess Athena, on the steps of her temple. I had entrusted myself to her once; I would do so again. My fate had been, from the very first, under her *aegis*.

I knew now what it took to bring something forth, glittering and alive, from the sun and the salt and the air. How will and desire entwined form something sinuous, greedy for life. My Pegasus, feathered and golden-edged. It lived within me, dormant and fettered, beside its brother, my glorious, giant Chryasor. He of the golden blade. The last of the great monsters, for a world unwilling to make room enough for us all.

The boy levelled the pointed edge of his sword at me. His arm trembled with the effort. On a day not so long ago, the trembling hands of a girl dipped into the dark water that closed over her, obscured her body below. She looked into the monstrous face of her desire and will, and saw what it would birth.

And so, I offered him what I had learned.

"There is room enough only in this world for will that is your own."

See Medusa lunge forward, their scaled coils taut with muscle seething, then surging and snapping. They snatch the hero's sword, holding it aloft.

"My goddess, Athena, I dedicate this birth to you! Let the world behold my children in their monstrous forms, my will and my desire entwined with the gods'. Let them reshape the world, so that the stories of gods and monsters—our stories—may never be forgotten."

And on the temple steps, before the cowering boy sent by a king to slay them, Medusa takes the sword and rends themselves in two, cleaving their own head from their neck.

A spray of blood mingles with seafoam, glittering and sunlit, on the sand.

From Medusa's neck springs Chryasor, the glorious giant, mounted on his twin Pegasus, a steed of pure and blinding white, a vision of flashing eyes and stone-flint hooves, and golden, feathered wings as broad as a girl's desire unfurled.

Mountain Sprout

by Cindy O'Quinn and Eugene Johnson

Beautiful woman, stone gardens and curses.

She'd been done wrong
    by one too many.
Now it was pain's song,
    she sang more than any.

A woman's rage, vengeance to make all wrongs right.

She used herbs, oils, and the old ways,
    straight from the weathered book.
Made no matter how many nights or days
    of hunting and trapping it took.

Mountain Medusa knew how to erase the haunted images with Nature and just one look.

She returned the pain, men eagerly gave,
    and she received what was left of their soul.
Each kill opened a new grave,
    located atop her skull, a hole.

The prize was power made of snakes, which sprouted from inside out, and held in place like hair.

Circus of Shadows

by Alyson Faye

The mist rolled in off the Thames, soupy and stinking, stretching out tentacles, smothering the city's inhabitants and shrouding the arrival of Emeritus Basculus' Circus of Shadows. Only a train of devoted street urchins followed the carnies' carts, whooping and jigging, begging for work and scraps of food.

The carnies handed out flyers to the ragamuffins, along with handfuls of pennies. Bare, bloodied feet scampered away into the sewage rich alleyways. Basculus rode in the largest covered wagon, up high, wrapped in a black velvet cape, his girth straining the fabric. In the recesses behind him something hissed and the canvas covering wriggled. The young lad, one Edwin Batley, whose sole job was to guard the exhibit, whispered, "Oy, Mr. B. it's moving again. I sure don't like this job."

His boss ignored him. In his head he was already counting the mountain of money this latest prize would bring. He'd be the richest man in the country soon, next to the blessed Queen Victoria herself.Several hours later, the carnies pitched the cavalcade of tents, creating a canvas kingdom on the bank of the River Thames. Eager customers flowed in, buying tickets and hot pasties, tossing hoopla and gawking at the Siamese Twins, Mr Yin and Mr Yang.

The longest queue gathered outside an elaborate wood framed construction. Above it the banner proclaimed, 'Myth or Monster? Goddess or Gorgon?'

Basculus sat outside, beneath the banner, on a hastily erected throne, newly-painted gold, smiling and pulling in the punters.

"Roll up, shows on the hour, every hour. Come and see the legend, the marvel which is … Medusa. Dare to stare into her eyes! A hundred guineas for the brave fella or lass who does, and lives to tell the tale. Pet the snakes, for a penny a stroke. She is here, one evening only, for the delight and delectation of all of London. Brought to you at great expense from the shores of Greece, from the waters of the Aegean Sea where she lay drowned for millennia."

A scuffle, shoving and heated words interrupted the showman's spiel. He frowned, "What's that you say, sir? A con? A fake? How dare YOU?" Basculus rose to his full height, six foot three, and towered above his audience. "The Circus of Shadows always delivers full value and total authenticity. I myself vouch for Medusa's pedigree." The crowd shuffled, no one wanted to challenge the circus owner—his height and girth were off-putting enough.

"First show is at eight. Buy your tickets at the booth. Ticket entry only, my friends." Basculus strode off the platform, sweeping his black cloak around him, and disappearing behind the curtains. "Is she ready?"

Edwin checked the ropes holding the canvas in place, for the hundredth time. The questing head of a snake peeked out from a corner, and the lad whipped his hand away just in time. Basculus lashed out with his silver topped cane, and whatever was under the canvas shrieked in pain or fury; it was not clear which.

"Make sure the mirrors are in situ and secured," Basculus instructed. "Tonight is the night we become millionaires." Edwin eyed the heaving, hissing mound with mixed emotions. He believed his boss' grandiose plan to be a catastrophe in the making. But who would listen to him? He'd been hired as a wrangler, not an advisor.

"Dunno bout Myth," Edwin muttered, "but you're definitely a monster."

The crowd at eight o'clock was double the usual in number, vociferous, and teetering on a knife-edge of violence. Edwin, watching from behind the side curtains, shivered. He didn't like the mood out there.

He'd learned, over the previous months as the creature's warder, several tricks to lull it. One was to sing lullabies, which his own late mother had sung to him, but with his own variations: *'Rock-a-bye, monster, on the sea top. When the wave soars, your sail boat will rock ...'*

He'd noticed how his singing lulled the snakes too, for they swayed in accompaniment. He found their movement hypnotic. She'd tricked him that way once at the beginning, but never again. Now he had her measure.

Edwin heard Basculus at the front of the stage, whipping the crowd even more into a frenzy. "You've all heard of Medusa, slain by Perseus? Of how he took her head, and gifted it to Athena who affixed it to her shield—the Gorgoneion."

The crowd grew restive at the history lesson. They had come for freaks and fun not education.

"C'mon bring the monster out."

"You're stalling. You ain't got nothing to show."

"Liar, cheater, trickster."

Bascalus silenced them, waving his cane, as though they were naughty school children. He turned and hit the brass gong placed by the throne and as the sound died away, a team of carnies, guided by Edwin, rolled the wheeled platform bearing the canvas mound out onto the stage, placing it squarely between the three mirrors.

"Untie the ropes," Basculus instructed. "Behold the eighth wonder of the world—the Gorgon known as Medusa. Be warned, good people, do NOT look into her eyes, only gaze upon her reflection in the mirrors."

Edwin lifted the canvas off his charge, and left her exposed to the eyes of the audience beneath the gas lights and the flames of the torches, so naked and vulnerable. He felt a frisson of pity for her, out here away from her natural watery habitat. Her reflection shimmered in the triple mirrors, as the eels wriggled and hissed, frantic to escape but tethered to her skull. She waved her flippers, tucked beneath her tiny belly, whilst her flat, sexless chest heaved in terror at the sight of so many people.

But it was her eyes that devastated Edwin, for each time he looked into them it broke his heart. When she sang, the notes as pure as crystal, touched him at his innermost core, and turned her into a creature of such beauty, it brought tears to his own eyes. He would do anything for her whilst she sang - lay down his life, fight for her, kill for her. He feared the reaction of the audience, for she was opening her mouth ...

He and Basculus reached for their ear mufflers, securing them hastily in place. Just in time. She began the opening notes of the lullaby of her own kind—lilting, languorous, romantic. The men in the audience began to sway, in time with her headful of dusky eels. The women sobbed, chests heaving, and the children rocked and danced as though they were drunk.

Next the men began to shove and push, skirmishes broke out, and the quicksilver of knife blades flashed. A child screamed, but fell abruptly silent. Edwin saw he'd been trampled beneath his parents' oblivious boots. A woman, wailing, ripped her clothes and hair. Her friends did the same, so that hanks of hair and scalp lay in the dirt. Others scratched at their chests and faces with their nails. Men threw punches at their neighbours, swearing and shouting, whilst the violence escalated and grew rampant. Blood spattered the stage and the red curtains and Edwin's boots.

Still the siren sang on—a unique, visceral tale of her long life and brutal abduction. No man present understood, but all felt her pain.

Edwin thought then that being turned to stone by the real Medusa might be preferable to this song-induced madness?

Basculus waited another minute, then nodded at Edwin. "Time to stop. They've had their money's worth." Edwin tossed the canvas over the creature, and her head of swarming eels, who hissed in defiance. The last echoing notes bled into the crowd's uproar, then faded. The crowd stilled.

"Didn't I say, folks, you'd get a good show for your money? Isn't she amazing? An eighth wonder of the world? One you will never forget?" Basculus boomed at the crowd who were coming to, as if sobering up, and gazing around themselves in confusion, drifted away into the night, barely speaking, stunned. The parents picked up their child's dead body, but with no emotion.

Edwin watching them and their blank faces, shuddered. He gazed at his boss. "Who's the monster here?"

The circus owner loomed over him. "Feed the eels, and get ready for the next show."

Basculus turned away, swaggering, vast girth swinging. King of the Stage. Edwin, a foot shorter, but agile and wiry, shoved the siren's platform at him with all his force, catching the man at the ankles. Basculus staggered, wobbled and nearly fell, but he regained his balance. Shouting obscenities, he turned to face Edwin, but the lad grabbed a lit torch and pushed the man in the middle of his chest. The flames leapt and fed greedily on the velvet of the cloak whilst the momentum of the push took him backwards off the stage into the dirt, where the dead child had lain minutes before.

Basculus, ablaze, screamed and floundered. Edwin watched from above, until the burning man was but a charcoal scarecrow. Edwin turned to the creature. "It is done. Now you are mine—forever."

Modern Medusa. © 2022 Chaz Kemp. All rights reserved.

Medi's Dance

by Jeanne E. Bush

She always wore sunglasses when she went out dancing.

Medusa—Medi to her acquaintances—never felt more free than when she was at the club. The lights flashing, the bass pounding, and everybody moving as one to the beat made her feel like she was a part of a greater whole. Accepted. People around her gave her space—possibly because of the wild snakes whirling in the air around her head—but no one seemed to mind and most seemed to think she was just a cool chick out having a good time.

New York City fit her well. By using sorcery and magic, she relocated here from the Old City a year ago, escaping her past. NYC embraced her, made her feel normal again. New Yorkers admired those with unique styles, so Medi felt at home as soon as she stepped off the plane. No one cared about her pasty, cracked green skin. No one batted an eye that instead of normal everyday hair, snakes covered her entire head. She found that feeding the snakes before heading out to run her errands made them sleepy, so they napped while she moved about the city. She thought the serpent hairdo gave her a distinctively hip style.

When she'd arrived in the city, she found a small but clean apartment and furnished it sparsely. Lonely at first, she adopted a cat named Athens for company.

She forgot about her curse for a moment and looked directly at the poor little thing. It instantly turned to stone, and she'd wept over it. She still had the kitty statue sitting on her small fireplace mantle. It made her feel so terrible that she never considered getting another pet. So she began to paint, to fill in the time and stave off the loneliness. They were crazy canvases showing the

Old City but with a New York stylishness. The freedom she felt when she painted made her feel alive again. She worked through a lot of the anger she still felt and released it into her artistry. Someday she hoped one of the boutique art galleries in the area might display them for her. For now, though, they were simply her escape.

Medi tried to forget about the past as she walked the streets of New York. It was tough at first, having lost her beautiful looks, her golden hair, and fair skin. She'd been so pampered in the Old City and hadn't wanted for a thing. After her brief affair with Poseidon, and the curse placed on her by Athena, she felt she was a victim who was punished unfairly. It shocked her to see the change in her appearance and to realize that she was no longer wanted or needed in the Old City. They ostracized her until she knew she had to escape.

It took a lot of time to let it all go, to embrace her new look and her new life. Now she was part of the buzz of the city, and she grew to truly appreciate it. Although she didn't have friends—after the kitty incident she felt it was too dangerous to ever have friends—she managed to make a good life for herself, and the community embraced her for her individuality.

But she had to be cautious. There were still warriors from the Old City who wanted her head. Not long ago, she experienced a close call and needed to use her abilities to save herself. She knew the man was following her, so led him into an alley. He thought he'd trapped her and brought out the long dagger to take her head. But she simply removed her sunglasses and looked him in the eyes, and within seconds he turned into a statue, the ancient dagger resting in his stony hand. He was still standing in that alley as far as she knew. But there would be others, so she had to stay on guard.

Not tonight, though. This night was about pure freedom and fun—in the middle of the dance floor, sunglasses on, music pounding, snake-hair flying. Surrounded by the young people of New York, she could forget for a while that she once had been one of the chosen few in the Old City. Medi felt her future was bright. She had made it this far because she was strong, smart, and resilient. She was a survivor.

Lagniappe

Lagniappe

During a staff meeting one gloriously stormy night, the idea of having a section titled "Lagniappe" near the end of some of the works published by Brigids Gate Press was discussed. The staff unanimously voted in favor of the idea.

Lagniappe (pronounced LAN-yap) is an old New Orleans tradition where merchants give a little something extra along with every purchase. It's a way of expressing thanks and appreciation to customers.

The Lagniappe section might contain a short story, a small handful of poems, or a non-fiction piece. It might also feature a short novella. It may or may not be connected with the theme of the work.

The extra offering for this anthology is "The Octavia" by Agatha Andrews. This haunting, eerie tale about a captain and his ship captivated us when we read it, and we knew we had to share it with all of our readers.

Enjoy!

The Octavia

by Agatha Andrews

Nicolas heard her voice on the wind.

"You dare return?" she whispered. The breeze whipped her words across his face, and he felt every lash. Though he tried to ignore it, he knew better. The Octavia was the only ghost he couldn't outrun. He risked crossing these waters again for the money, just as he burned and sank his ship ten years ago for the riches that awaited him, a pay-off from a merchant competing with the owner of the cargo he carried. Though he owned The Octavia outright, the money was worth her sacrifice.

"You aren't real," he said his voice raspy with guilt.

She laughed.

Nicolas scanned the deck to see if the other men heard her sharp cackle, but they all scurried about like ants after a child kicked their mound, busy and focused on their work.

"Save your bravado, you fool," she mocked. "I can feel your fear churning through the water like a storm across the sea."

His heart rattled in his chest like a thunderclap. He knew a boat was not a living thing, but many captains swore that each ship had a soul. Until this moment, he hadn't been sure. He avoided these waters for years, afraid of his past that lurked in the depths, but his greed took a gamble he now regretted.

"Octavia," he whispered, like a mournful lover, filled with a sorrow of his own making. Through several raging tempests, she never failed Nicolas. She stayed upright through every thunderous wave that tried to bring her down, her warrior spirit ignited by the bond she believed they had. He carved her figurehead, spent

months perfecting her face, her breasts, her gown that appeared to flutter against her thighs as she perched on the ship's prow. He carved eyes into her face that were at once serene and fierce, and they stayed ever vigilant as she charged forward on each voyage. He loved The Octavia, but not enough.

"I'm sorry," he said, though he knew it was too late.

The wind carried no reply. It stopped blowing at all.

The crew dropped their work and rushed to the side of the ship when a fellow sailor called on them to look overboard. Nicolas stayed behind. He had no wish to gaze on the wreckage. The water was so clear it almost wasn't blue, and they marveled at The Octavia's shadow through the deep, quiet sea, a charred and broken vessel resting in a watery grave.

The men silently fixated on the haunting image, praying for the sailors lost during her tragic end. They couldn't see the eyes staring up at them from the figure, broken off the bow, laying on the sandy floor.

"Alright, lads," Nicolas said, not acknowledging his connection to the sunken boat. "You've not noticed the wind has died and we have work to do if we are to get past the doldrum."

The crew resumed bustling about on the borrowed boat. He was now in the business of getting other men's cargo from one place to the next with no commitment to the vessel. It was easier to abandon ship that way, when necessary, like a string of meaningless lovers after forsaking a wife.

"There won't be a moon tonight," Nicolas said to his helmsman as the sky grew dark.

"I'll be fine, Captain. Get some sleep," the helmsman said. "I have faith the winds will return. You've nothing to worry about."

Famous last words, Nicolas thought. He said nothing, but walked around the ship, unsure of what to look for. Though he dared not look over the rails, the greedy part of him wondered what valuables still lay buried in the wreckage taunting him from below. He knew it didn't matter. He could do nothing about it. Then he wondered if the Octavia's ghost heard that thought, and he cursed himself for it.

"Are you there?" he asked out into the wind, tentative and tired from worry, but she did not reply. Water sloshed melodically against the sides of the boat, and everything seemed at peace. Perhaps he imagined it all. Satisfied, Nicolas patted his hand on the ship's railing as if rewarding a delighted dog, and shuffled off to his cabin. Consumed by exhaustion, he fell asleep as his head met his pillow.

Octavia didn't wait long.

"Nicolas," she whispered like a quiet lullaby against his ear.

He felt her breath on his skin, and it cut through him like a blade made of ice. His eyes flew open, and he knew at once the phantom woman that stood before him. The ghost of his sunken ship took the figurehead's form. He trembled, remembering how he kissed her mouth, licked her breast, and rutted himself against her time and again while she was still a wooden figure hidden in his workshop. She could move now, no longer trapped in a wooden body. She had free will and anger. Nicolas had never seen anything more dangerous.

"You used to think me beautiful," she said through lips that were now cracked and peeling. "But only when no one was looking." Water puddled on the floor around her feet. She stood as proud and fearless as she once did at the bow of his boat. "I remember everything you did to me, but I feel things differently now." She gave him a sly look, gently caressing the delicate tips of her breasts with her fingertips. "Would you like to do those things again? I want to feel what it's like in my new body."

Nicolas felt the churning in his gut but dared not show it. He sat up in bed, pulling his blanket around him, as if it could protect him from a ghost that emerged from the deep. Her sharp eyes once guided him across oceans. Now they pierced through him like a flaming arrow. He gaped at her skin, split and barnacled from lying broken beneath the sea.

"You loved me once," she said moving closer to him, "but now you tremble in horror."

"I love you still," he said, his voice quaking with the lie.

231

She reached her soggy hand to his face, dripping salty water down his cheek like tears. "Is that so?" she asked.

He fought back the bile of revulsion pushing its way up from his gut as she put her lips to his. She tasted like burnt wood and watery rot.

"Did you come back for me then?" she asked.

"I ... want to," he struggled to say. "But you know that I can't." He lifted his hand to hers and shuttered at the slimy texture of her skin. His eyes grew wide as he saw the fine strands of green algae adhered to her like tiny, greasy hairs. As he jerked his hand back, he brushed against the hard barnacles hidden between her fingers, and he could hold back no more. He retched over the side of the bed.

The ghost took several deep breaths, fast and full of gurgling fury, as though she was fighting not to drown all over again. She grabbed Nicolas, still hunched and panting over his bile, and yanked his head back by his hair. Inches from his face, she glared at him. "You should have died with me ... *Captain*."

Nicolas felt the spit of the last word like a slap on the face. Captains are not supposed to abandon ship, but he did, as he always knew he would. He hired men who didn't know they were damned. Some were little more than boys on their first pass across the ocean. It was easier to dispose of a less capable crew. Now, their hopes and their futures lay buried in the water, along with whatever remained of their bodies, and he realized they might be waiting for him too.

"I'm ... I'm so sorry," he sputtered. Cold water trickled down his back and he had no idea if it was cold sweat or water dripping from her wet hands as she held his head with a grip that still threatened to break his neck. A slight twist was all it would take.

Her cracked lips curled into a terrifying smile. "Prove it," she said, water sliding out of the corners of her mouth.

"I don't know how," Nicolas said as his body grew suddenly cold, as though he were plunging to the bottom of an arctic sea. He couldn't move. All he could do was weep.

"Oh, I think you do," she gurgled.

Nicolas whimpered as she pressed her lips against his, their mouths slurping with his bile and her salty water. It was the last thing he tasted when she sucked the life from him. As she pulled him beneath the water that night, his dead eyes stared up into a moonless sky, no trails of light shining in farewell. When she reached her wreckage, the ghost of The Octavia thrust him into her dark caverns and gave him to the waiting souls that once did their best to save her.

Afterword

Tempered Tales was supposed to be an online literary magazine. The idea was born during the *Musings of the Muses* submissions call in 2021. The stories and poems about Medusa far outnumbered all others. We thought in 2022 we would launch the magazine and the first issue would be all about Medusa in order to include some of the work we'd received. We were a little short on the word count we wanted, so we opened a short sub call in order to capture a couple more stories and a handful of poems. Word traveled fast and we received an enormous number of submissions. The magazine quickly changed to an anthology. We plan to release a *Tempered Tales Anthology* volume every other year. Each volume will be stories and poems of one character, like Medusa, instead of a general theme.

Heather Vassallo
September 2022

About the Authors

Eva Papasoulioti is a writer of speculative fiction and poetry. She lives in Athens, Greece, with her spouse and their two cats, and translates words for a living. Her work has appeared in *Uncanny Magazine*, *Star*Line*, *Syntax & Salt*, *Polu Texni* and elsewhere. You can find her on twitter @epapasoulioti and on her blog plothopes.com.

Laura G. Kaschak was born and raised in the pine barrens of New Jersey where she spent most of her youth hanging out with the Jersey devil. Now she is a wife and mother of two in Virginia successfully fooling everyone into believing she is a grown up. When she's not writing, she's working on her latest art creation or Halloween costume.

Linda D. Addison, the author of five award-winning collections, including *The Place of Broken Things* written with Alessandro Manzetti, & *How To Recognize A Demon Has Become Your Friend*, recipient of the HWA Lifetime Achievement Award and SFPA Grand Master of Fantastic Poetry.

SJ Townend is the twist you never expected. She is also a writer of odd, dark tales and lives in Bristol, UK with her family. She's had work published with Brigids Gate Press, Sunbury Press, Timber Ghost Press, Ghost Orchid Press, and Gravely Unusual Magazine amongst others, and right now, she's busy compiling her first collection of horror stories, working title: *Sick Girl Screams*, so she may not answer the phone if it rings.

Christina Sng is the two-time Bram Stoker Award-winning author of *A Collection of Dreamscapes* (2020) and *A Collection of Nightmares*(2017). Her fiction has appeared in *Black Cranes: Tales of Unquiet Women, Daily Science Fiction, Fantastic Stories of the Imagination,* and *Space and Time*. Visit her at christinasng.com and connect @christinasng.

Ann Wuehler has four novels out, *Oregon Gothic* and *House on Clark Boulevard, Aftermath: Boise, Idaho* and *The Remarkable Women of Brokenheart Lane*. A short story, "Man and Mouse", appears in the April 2020 issue of *Sun* magazine. Her play, *Bluegrass of God*, is in Santa Ana River Review. Her short story, "Jimmy's Jar Collection", appeared in the *Ghastling's 13* and her "The Little Visitors" was in the *Ghastling's 10*. She has five stories placed with "Whistle Pig", "Maybelle", "Bunny Slipper", "Pearlie at the Gates of Dawn", "Greenhorn and Elbow and Bean". "City Full of Rain" debuted in *Litmag*. "Gladys", a short story, appeared in *Agony Opera*. The short story, the "Elephant Girl", was in the September 2021's the *Bosphorus Review*. "Pig Bait" has been included in *Gore*, an anthology by Poe Boy Publishing, back in October 2021. The "Witch of the Highway", a short story, appeared in the *World of Myth* in October 2021 as well. "Blood and Bread" will appear in Hellbound Books' *Toilet Zone 3, the Royal Flush*, due out in 2022. "Lilith's Arm" just got an acceptance from Bag of Bones, to be included in their 2022 *Annus Horribilis* anthology. The "Salty Monkey Mystery", a short story, will also be published for a charity anthology.

Amanda Steel is an author, poet, podcast co-host and copywriter from Manchester. She co-hosts the book review podcast *Reading in Bed*. Her books include, *Ghost of Me* (which was a finalist in the Author Elite 2020 awards), two full length poetry books, and several chapbooks. She has also edited two anthologies; *From the Shadows*, and *Words to Remember*. Amanda's poetry has been broadcast on BBC Radio Manchester, and her story, "Clown Control" was featured on *The NoSleep Podcast*.

Her blog is: amandasteelwriter.wordpress.com

Ellie Detzler is an author dedicated to writing tales of adventure and romance. She has been an avid writer since she was a child, writing swashbuckling tales of pirates. Now the pirates and swashbucklers are predominately gay women in love with each other. Ellie enjoys little more than weaving stories of Lady Knights saving Princesses, and adventurers finding comfort in each other's arms after a battle by the roadside. When not writing, Ellie enjoys reading and is an avid gardener, growing simple herbal remedies.

Elizabeth Davis is a second generation writer living in Dayton, Ohio. They live there with their spouse and two cats - neither of which have been lost to ravenous corn mazes or sleeping serpent gods. they can be found at deadfishbooks.com when they aren't busy creating beautiful nightmares and bizarre adventures. Their work can be found at *Illumen1*, *All Worlds Wayfarer*, and *Sci Fi Lampoon*.

Katherine Silva is a Maine author of dark fiction, a connoisseur of coffee, and victim of cat shenanigans. She is a two-time Maine Literary Award finalist for speculative fiction and a member of the Horror Writers of Maine, The Horror Writers Association, and New England Horror Writers Association. Katherine is also a founder of Strange Wilds Press and Dark Taiga Creative Writing Consultations. Her latest book, *The Wild Dark*, is now available wherever books are sold.

Megan Baffoe is an emerging freelance writer currently pursuing English Language and Literature at Oxford University. She likes fairytales, fraught family dynamics, and unreliable narration; she does not like Twitter, but may be found @meginageorge. All of her published work is available at meganspublished.tumblr.com.

Rachel Horak Dempsey has written and directed over a dozen plays for numerous acclaimed theater organizations such as *Imagination Stage* and *ArtStream*. Her prose won first prize in *The Colorado Gold Rush Literary Awards* and also won the *Denver Women's Press Club Emerging Writers Contest*. Her dark fiction is forthcoming with Shacklebound Books and Brigids Gate Press (*Daughter of Sarpedon* anthology). She holds a BFA in Drama and English from NYU's Tisch School of the Arts and a Master's degree in Journalism from Georgetown University. Currently, she lives in Denver with her husband and three daughters and attends the MFA program at Regis, studying with mentors Jenny Shank, Erika T. Wurth and David Heska Wanbli Weiden. She also participates in the writing community and hones her craft through Lighthouse Writers Workshop and Rocky Mountain Fiction Writers. Find her on Instagram at @rachelsuedempsey, on Twitter @rachelsdempsey and blogging at www.rmfw.org/blog.

Romy Tara Wenzel lives on Melukerdee country, Tasmania, exploring mythology and ecology from an animist perspective. Her preoccupation is with liminal states: the spaces between becoming and unbecoming, wildness and domesticity, inter-species communication and ecstatic transformation. Recent publications include short stories in *Dark Mountain*, *Hecate*, *Cunning Folk*, and *Folklore for Resistance*.

Stephanie M. Wytovich is an American poet, novelist, and essayist. Her work has been showcased in numerous magazines and anthologies such as *Weird Tales*, *Nightmare Magazine*, *Southwest Review*, *Year's Best Hardcore Horror: Volume 2*, *The Best Horror of the Year: Volume 8*, as well as many others.

Stephanie M. Wytovich is the Poetry Editor for Raw Dog Screaming Press, an adjunct at Western Connecticut State University, Southern New Hampshire University, and Point Park University, and a mentor with Crystal Lake Publishing. She is a recipient of the 2021 Ladies of Horror Fiction Writers Grant and has received the Rocky Wood Memorial Scholarship for non-fiction writing.

Wytovich is a member of the Science Fiction Poetry Association, an active member of the Horror Writers Association, and a graduate of Seton Hill University's MFA program for Writing Popular Fiction. Her Bram Stoker Award-winning poetry collection, *Brothel*, earned a home with Raw Dog Screaming Press alongside *Hysteria: A Collection of Madness*, *Mourning Jewelry*, *An Exorcism of Angels*, *Sheet Music to My Acoustic Nightmare*, and most recently, *The Apocalyptic Mannequin*. Her debut novel, *The Eighth*, is published with Dark Regions Press.

Follow Wytovich at stephaniewytovich.blogspot.com and on Twitter and Instagram @SWytovich and @thehauntedbookshelf. You can also find her essays, nonfiction, and class offerings on LitReactor.

Die Booth lives in Chester, UK, and likes making monsters and exploring dark places. You can read his stories in places like *Lamplight Magazine*, *The Fiction Desk* and *Firewords*. His books *My Glass is Runn*, *365 Lies* (profits go to the MNDA) and *Spirit Houses* are available online and he's currently working on a collection of spooky stories featuring transgender protagonists.

diebooth.wordpress.com/ @diebooth

Rachel Rixen lives in Fargo, ND with her two cats. She enjoys writing fiction that's about as short as her attention span and fills in the rest of her time with crochet, baking and freelance work.

See more of her work or contact her at:
rrixwriter.journoportfolio.com

Federica Santini lives in Atlanta and teaches at Kennesaw State University. She holds an MA from the University of Siena, Italy, and a PhD from UCLA. She has authored or edited four volumes on poetics and her work has been published internationally in over forty journals and anthologies. An immigrant writer, she uses English towards freedom.

Thomas Joyce lives in his hometown near Glasgow, Scotland with his wife and daughter. He has had short stories published at thehorrorzine.com, in *Unnerving Magazine*, and *Lost Films*, ananthology published by Perpetual Motion Machine Publishing in 2018. His latest publication was a flash fiction story at guiltycrimemag.com in July 2021. "A Strongly-Worded Email About the Ghost in Our Motorhome" will soon be appearing on the podcast, *Thirteen*.

L. Minton (she/her) is a queer poet living in the American South. She shares a home with her mother, son, and a spooky cat, and has tried most jobs at least once.

Catherine McCarthy is a Welsh writer of dark tales with macabre melodies. She is the author of the short story collections *Door and other twisted tales* and *Mists and Megaliths*, and the novella, *Immortelle*, published by Off Limits Press July 2021. Her work has been published by Brigids Gate Press, Gallery for the Curious, and Black Spot Books. When she is not writing she may be found hiking the Welsh coast path or huddled among ancient gravestones reading Machen or Poe. Discover more at www.catherine-mccarthy-author.com or, alternatively at twitter.com/serialsemantic.

Ai Jiang is a Chinese-Canadian writer, an immigrant from Fujian, and an active member of HWA. Her work has appeared or is forthcoming in *F&SF*, *The Dark*, *Dark Matter*, *PseudoPod*, *Uncanny*, *The Deadlands*, among others. Find her on Twitter (@AiJiang_) and online (http://aijiang.ca).

Katie Young is a writer of dark fiction. Her work appears in various anthologies including collections by Scott J. Moses, Nyx Publishing, Ghost Orchid Press, and Fox Spirit Books, and her story, "Lavender Tea", was selected by Zoe Gilbert for inclusion in the Mechanic Institute Review's Summer Folk Festival 2019. She lives in West London with her partner, an angry cat, and too many books.

Lyndsey Croal is an Edinburgh-based writer of speculative and strange fiction. She is a Scottish Book Trust New Writers Awardee, and her work has been published in several anthologies and magazines, including Mslexia's *Best Women's Short Fiction 2021*. In 2021, her debut audio drama was produced by *Alternative Stories & Fake Realities*, and she is currently editing *Ghostlore: An Audio Fiction Anthology*, with the same podcast. Find her on Twitter as @writerlynds or via www.lyndseycroal.co.uk.

Elyse Russell is a writer of comics and short stories, and a curator of anthologies. She's been telling stories since she was kid, and wrote her first (terrible) novel when she was sixteen. 2021 was the year she finally decided to try to get published. When not writing, she enjoys long naps with her cats, reading, fashion design, and donuts. She loves to collaborate on projects, so feel free to contact her through email or Twitter if you have ideas! Some of her favorite writers: Edgar Allen Poe, Anne Rice, Brian K. Vaughn, Margaret Atwood, Tanith Lee, Gail Simone, George R. R. Martin, and Neil Gaiman.

Deborah Markus lives and works in Santa Monica, California, in an apartment populated entirely by authors and lizards. Her YA/suspense novel *The Letting Go* was described by Kirkus as "wonderfully eerie and disorienting." She is currently working on her next novel and occasionally posting at Aphantastic Writer (aphantasticwriter.com), a blog about her autism, aphantasia, and other neurodiversities.

April Yates is a writer of dark and queer fiction, living in Derbyshire England with her wife and two fluffy demons masquerading as dogs. She should be writing, but is easily distracted by the squirrels in her garden or thoughts of lesbian vampires. Her debut novella, *Ashthorne*, a queer, historical horror-romance will be published by Ghost Orchid Press in 2022. Her short stories appear in anthologies by Ghost Orchid Press, Brigids Gate Press and Black Hare Press. She also suffers from a micro-fiction addiction, leaving them scattered across the web and in various anthologies. Find her on Twitter @April_Yates_ or aprilyates.com.

Theresa Derwin writes Horror & dark comedy. She has over sixty anthology acceptances including the story "Shift Left for Love" in Brigid's Gate Press' *Weretales*. She has just achieved her MA Creative Writing.Theresa has published four collections and edited over ten anthologies. Her forthcoming books include *God's Vengeance* from Crystal Lake Publishing.Her latest #WIHM anthology is as one of a quartet of #WIH *Daughters of Darkness* from Black Angel Press.She is the 2019 HWA Mary Shelley Scholarship recipient. Follow her at

Twitter @BarbarellaFem and Instagram @theresa.derwinauthor.

Website under construction. Much life herself it is old and tired, requiring a face lift.

Jason P. Burnham writes words and poems that are occasionally published. He loves spending time with his family and cooking beans. He wishes cat allergies were curable in this timeline.

Twitter: @AndGalen email: burnhamjp@gmail.com

Claire McNerney is an actor, student, and writer from California, where she currently attends UCSD. She enjoys, among other things, the variety and shapes of clouds. Her writing has been previously published in Blue Marble Review and Wyldblood, and is forthcoming in Los Suelos. To keep in touch with her writing, check out her twitter: @claire_mcnerney.

Marisca Pichette is an author of speculative fiction, nonfiction, and poetry. Further work by her has been published and is forthcoming in *Strange Horizons*, *PseudoPod*, *Daily Science Fiction*, *Fireside*, *Uncharted*, and *PodCastle*, among others. A lover of moss and monsters, she lives in Western Massachusetts.

Twitter: @MariscaPichette

Instagram: @marisca_write

Website: www.mariscapichette.com

Gordon Linzner is founder and former editor of *Space and Time Magazine*, and author of three published novels and scores of short stories in *F&SF*, *Twilight Zone*, *Sherlock Holmes Mystery Magazine*, and numerous other magazines and anthologies. He is a member of the Horror Writers Association and a lifetime member of the Science Fiction & Fantasy Writers of America.

Patricia Gomes is the Poet Laureate of New Bedford, Massachusetts from 2014 to 2021, author and playwright Patricia Gomes is published in numerous literary journals and anthologies, including the New England Horror Writers Anthologies, *Wicked Women* and *Wicked Creatures*. A Pushcart Prize nominee in 2008, 2018 and 2021, and twice nominated for a Rhysling Science Fiction award, Gomes is the author of four chapbooks. Ms. Gomes recent publications include *Tidings*, *Star*Line*, *Muddy River Review*, *Motif Magazine*, *Alien Buddha Press*, and *Apex and Abyss*. Ms. Gomes is the co-founder of the GNB Writers Block as well a member of the Massachusetts Poetry Society, the SciFi Poetry Association, New England Horror Writers, the Horror Writers Association.

Stephen Frame lives by the sea. He read way too much Harlan Ellison at an early age and blames anything and everything that happened afterwards on that.

Sharmon Gazaway's work has appeared or is forthcoming in *The Forge Literary Magazine, MetaStellar, Daily Science Fiction, New Myths* (twice), *Enchanted Conversation, Ghost Orchid Press, Breath and Shadow* (twice), *Metaphorosis, and elsewhere*. You can also find her work in the anthologies *Daughter of Sarpedon, Orpheus + Eurydice Rewoven, Love Letters to Poe Volumes I* and *II, Wayward & Upward*, and, *Dark Waters*. Her work is nominated for the 2022 Dwarf Stars Award. Sharmon writes from the Deep South, where she lives beside a historic cemetery haunted by the wild cries of pileated woodpeckers. She is currently at work on an adult fantasy novel. You can follow her on Instagram at sharmongazaway.

Kayla Whittle works in acquisitions for a medical publisher. She has previously had a short story published in *Luna Station Quarterly* and *The Colored Lens*. Other stories appear in the anthologies *Beyond the Veil* published by Ghost Orchid Press and *Eros & Thanatos* by Crow & Quill Publishing. Most often she can be found on Instagram @caughtbetweenthepages or on Twitter @kaylawhitwrites. When not writing, she's usually busy reading, embroidering, or planning her next Disney vacation. She currently resides in New Jersey.

Instagram: caughtbetweenthepages

Twitter: kaylawhitwrites

Alexis DuBon is a work of fiction. Any resemblance to actual persons, living or dead, is purely coincidental. You can find her in *Field Notes From a Nightmare* by Dread Stone Press, *A Woman Built By Man* by Cemetery Gates Media, *A Quaint and Curious Volume of Gothic Tales* by Brigids Gate Press, and on twitter at @shakedubonbon.

Sam Muller loves books and dogs and spends much time trying to save one from the other. Her stories have appeared in several publications including *Cosmic Roots* and *Eldritch Shores*, *Voyage YA*, and the *Wyldblook Magazine*. Her first novel, a YA/fantasy cum murder mystery, will be published by Fractured Mirror publishing in October 2023.

Avra Margariti is a queer author, Greek sea monster, and Rhysling-nominated poet with a fondness for the dark and the darling. Avra's work haunts publications such as *Vastarien*, *Asimov's*, *Liminality*, *Arsenika*, *The Future Fire*, *Space and Time*, *Eye to the Telescope*, and *Glittership*. "The Saint of Witches", Avra's debut collection of horror poetry, is available from Weasel Press. You can find Avra on twitter (@avramargariti).

Christina Bagni has worked as a journalist with *The Boston Globe* and an editorial intern with *Ploughshares Literary Journal.* Her creative work has been published in *Asterism,Corridors,* and *Underground Literary Magazine,* and she is a fiction editor at Wandering Words Media. She is also a writer on the *Captain Bitcoin* comic book series.

Social Media Handles: Twitter: @ChristinaBagni, Facebook: www.facebook.com/cbagni

Kristin Cleaveland writes horror, dark fiction, and poetry. Her work has appeared in *Vastarien, Southwest Review, Black Telephone Magazine,* and more, including anthologies such as *Ravens & Roses: A Women's Gothic Anthology* from Quill and Crow Publishing House and *Musings of the Muses* from Brigid's Gate Press. She is an Affiliate Member of the Horror Writers Association. Find her on Twitter as @KristinCleaves.

Eric J. Guignard is a writer and anthologist of dark and speculative fiction, operating from the shadowy outskirts of Los Angeles. He's twice won the Bram Stoker Award, been a finalist for the International Thriller Writers Award, and a multi-nominee of the Pushcart Prize. His latest books are his novella *Last Case at a Baggage Auction* (Harper Day), novel *Doorways to the Deadeye* (JournalStone), and short story collection *That Which Grows Wild* (Cemetery Dance).Visit Eric at: www.ericjguignard.com or Twitter: @ericjguignard.

Marshall J. Moore is a writer, filmmaker, and martial artist born and raised on Kwajalein, a tiny Pacific Island. He has traveled to over twenty countries, once sold a thousand dollars' worth of teapots to Jackie Chan, and on one occasion was tracked down by a bounty hunter for owing $300 in late fees to the Los Angeles Public Library. An active member of the SFWA, his work has been published by Mysterion, Air and Nothingness Press, Flame

Tree, and many others. He lives in Atlanta, Georgia, with his wife Megan and their two cats.

Twitter: @Kwaj14 Instagram: @kwajmarshall

Facebook: www.facebook.com/kwajmarshall

Owl Goingback has been writing professionally for over thirty years, and is the author of numerous novels, children's book, screenplays, magazine articles, and short stories. He is a three-time Bram Stoker Award Winner, receiving the award for lifetime achievement, best novel, and best first novel. His books include *Crota, Darker Than Night, Evil Whispers, Breed, Shaman Moon, Coyote Rage, Eagle Feathers, Tribal Scream*s, and *The Gift*. In addition to writing under his own name, Owl has ghostwritten several books for Hollywood celebrities.

Renée Meloche (she/they/he) writes queer fiction and poetry when she's not hosting podcasts. Renée's short fiction has appeared in Prairie Soul Press' *Prairie Witch* anthology, and theirpoems have recently appeared in *Lita Literary* and *NoD Magazine*. Find more of Renée's work at reneewrought.com.

Cindy O'Quinn is an Appalachian writer who grew up in the mountains of West Virginia. In 2016, Cindy and her family moved to the northern woods of Maine, where she continues to write horror stories and speculative poetry. Her work has been published or is forthcoming in *Shotgun Honey Presents Vol 4: RECOIL*, The Shirley Jackson Award Winning Anthology: *The Twisted Book of Shadows, Shelved: Appalachian Resilience During Covid 19 Anthology, Attack From The '80s Anthology, The Bad Book Anthology, Chiral Mad 5, HWA Poetry Showcase Vol V, Space & Time Magazine, Weirdbook Magazine, Nothing's Sacred Vol 4 & 5, Sanitarium Magazine*, & others. Cindy is a two-time Bram Stoker Award Final Nominee. Her poetry has been nominated for both the Rhysling

& Dwarf Star Awards. Member of HWA, NESW, NEHW, SFPA, Horror Writers of Maine, and Weird Poets Society. You can follow Cindy for updates on:

Facebook @CindyOQuinnWriter, Instagram cindy.oquinn, and Twitter @COQuinnWrites.

Bram Stoker Award®-winner **Eugene Johnson** is a bestselling editor, author and columnist. He has written as well as edited in various genres, and created anthologies such as the Fantastic Tales of Terror, Drive in Creature Feature with Charles Day, the Bram Stoker Award®-nominated nonfiction anthology Where Nightmares Come From: The Art of Storytelling in the Horror Genre and many more. As a filmmaker, Eugene Johnson worked on various movies, including the upcoming Requiem, starring Tony Todd and directed by Paul Moore. His short film Leftovers, a collaboration with director Paul Moore, was featured at the Screamfest Film Festival in Los Angeles as well as Dragoncon. Eugene is currently a member of the Horror Writers Association. He resides in West Virginia with his partner Angela, daughter, and two sons.

Alyson Faye lives in the UK, with her family; she works as a tutor, editor and proofreader. She is currently co-editor on thecasket.co.uk. Her work has appeared in varied anthologies and e-zines. Most recently in *Space and Time* #141, *Coffin Bell Journal*, *Night Frights 2* from Perpetual Motion Press, and Kandisha Press' *Don't Break the Oath.'*

Her fiction has been read out on BBC Radio, local radio and several podcasts e.g. Ladies of Horror. She enjoys outdoor swimming, old movies, and is often to be found on the moor with her rescue Lab, Roxy.

www.amazon.co.uk/kindle-dbs/entity/author/B01NBYSLRT

Jeanne E. Bush is a writer whose fiction includes the story *Off the Beaten Path*, published in the anthology *206-Word Stories* (Bag of Bones Press), the story *Wheels* which appears in the anthology *CHROMOPHOBIA: A Strangehouse Anthology by Women in Horror* (Rooster Republic Press/Strangehouse Books), and the story "Medi's Dance" which will be published in the anthology *Daughter of Sarpedon* (Brigid's Gate Press). She lives with her family in Oregon. You can follow her on Twitter @jeannelene.

Agatha Andrews is a writer and podcaster that lurks in libraries and historic cemeteries. She writes spooky Texas history for magazines and talks to authors about their gothic fiction on the *She Wore Black Podcast*. You can find her on Twitter and Instagram, and listen to her show wherever you get your podcasts.

Twitter - @AgathaAWrites or @SheWoreBlackPod

Instagram – @agathaandrewsauthor or @sheworeblackpodcast

Website – www.sheworeblackpodcast.com

About the Editors

Heather Vassallo, co-founder of Brigids Gate Press, believes there are few things that can't be solved with tea, cookies, and a good book. Like nature, she abhors a vacuum. She enjoys reading a wide range of genres, but can't resist fairytales and gothic novels. She currently resides with her husband, son, and two horribly mischievous black cats under the vast prairie skies of the Midwest. She continues to believe the world is a place full of magic and wonder (and lost shakers of salt).

www.brigidsgatepress.com
Twitter: @BrigidsGate
Instagram: @brigidsgatepress

S.D. Vassallo is a co-founder and editor for Brigids Gate Press, LLC. He's also a writer who loves horror, fantasy, science fiction and crime fiction. He was born and raised in New Orleans, but currently lives in the Midwest with his wife, son, and two black cats who refuse to admit that coyotes exist. When not reading, writing or editing, he can be found gazing at the endless skies of the wide-open prairie. He often spends the night outdoors when the full moon is in sway.

www.brigidsgatepress.com
Twitter: @diovassallo and @BrigidsGate
Instagram: @s.d.vassallo
www.sdvassallo.com

About the Illustrator

Elizabeth Leggett is a Hugo award-winning illustrator whose work focuses on soulful, human moments-in-time that combine ambiguous interpretation and curiosity with realism.

Much to her mother's dismay, she viewed her mother's white washed walls as perfectly good canvasses so she believes it is safe to say that she has been an artist her whole life! Her first published work was in the Halifax County Arts Council poetry and illustration collection. If she remembers correctly, she was not yet in double digits yet, but she might be wrong about that. Her first paying gig was painting other students' tennis shoes in high school.

In 2012, she ended a long fallow period by creating a full seventy-eight card tarot in a single year. From there, she transitioned into freelance illustration. Her clients represent a broad range of outlets, from multiple Hugo award winning Lightspeed Magazine to multiple Lambda Literary winner, Lethe Press. She was honored to be chosen to art direct both Women Destroy Fantasy and Queers Destroy Science Fiction, both under the Lightspeed banner.

Elizabeth, her husband, and their typically atypical cats, live in New Mexico. She suggests if you ever visit the state, look up. The skies are absolutely spectacular!

Content Warnings

Sledgehammer by Ann Wuehler: domestic abuse, trauma flashback

A Lullaby from the Old World by Katherine Silva: blood, murder, death, snakes, body horror

Hunger by Megan Baffoe: murder

Gods and Other Monsters by Rachel Horak Dempsey: violence, intended rape

Snakehair by Romy Tara Wenzel: implied rape

Sanctuary by Catherine McCarthy: death

A Tongueless Daughter by Ai Jiang: death, murder

Sea Change by Katie Young: implied rape

The Original Nasty Woman by Theresa Derwin: attempted rape

Down on the Lower East Side by Stephen Frame: implied abuse

Don't Tell Me to Smile by Kristin Cleaveland: sexual assault

Firsts by Marshall J. Moore: implied attempted assault

Circus of Shadows by Alyson Faye: brief reference to child death

More from Brigids Gate Press

Visit our website at: www.bridgidsgatepress.com

Paperback ISBN: 978-1-957537-05-4

Arthur, whose life was devastated by the brutal murder of his wife, must come to terms with his diagnosis of dementia. He moves into a new home at retirement community, and shortly after, has his life turned upside down again when his wife's ghost visits him and sends him on a quest to find her killer so her spirit can move on. With his family and his doctor concerned that his dementia is advancing, will he be able to solve the murder before his independence is permanently restricted?

A Man in Winter examines the horrors of isolation, dementia, loss, and the ghosts that come back to haunt us.

Paperback ISBN: 978-1-957537-10-8

During the Spring Equinox underneath London, four people enter the caves, but only one will survive. Each trespasser must battle their own demons before facing the White Lady who rises each year to feed on human flesh.

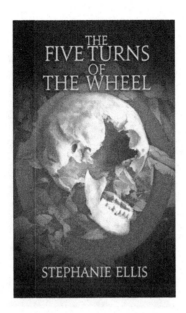

Paperback ISBN: 978-1-957537-21-4

Welcome to the Weald.
The Five Turns of the Wheel has begun.
With each Turn, blood will be spilled,
and sacrifices will be made.
Pacts will be made … and broken.
Will you join the Dance?

In the Weald, the time has come for The Five Turns of the Wheel.
Tommy, Betty and Fiddler, the sons of Hweol, Lord of Umbra,
have arrived to oversee the sacred rituals … rituals brimming with
sacrifice and dripping with blood.
Megan Wheelborn, daughter of Tommy, hatches a desperate plan
to free the people of the Weald from the bloody and cruel grip of
Umbra, and put an end to its murderous rituals. But success will
require sacrifice and blood as well. Will Megan be able to pay the
price?

Paperback ISBN: 978-1-957537-31-3

Stewartville. A town living in the shadow of the prisons that drive its economy. Haunted by the ghosts of its past. Cursed by the dark secrets hidden beneath. A town so entwined with the prisons waiting outside the city limits that it's impossible to imagine one without the other, or to ever imagine escaping either.

When a teenage boy digs into the history of the town, he discovers a tunnel system beneath Stewartville, passageways filled with dark secrets. Secrets leaning not to freedom but to unrelenting terror.

Stewartville. Where the convicts aren't the only prisoners

Made in the USA
Coppell, TX
16 December 2022